D0627117

Relatively Dangerous

RODERIC JEFFRIES

Relatively Dangerous

An Inspector Alvarez novel

St. Martin's Press
New York

Library of Congress Cataloging-in-Publication Data

Jeffries, Roderic, 1926–
        Relatively dangerous.

        I. Title.
PR6060.E43R4   1987   823′.914   87-7236
ISBN 0-312-01080-X

First published in Great Britain by William Collins Sons &
Co., Ltd.

First U.S. Edition

10   9   8   7   6   5   4   3   2   1

Relatively Dangerous

CHAPTER 1

The lower slopes on either side of the deep, twisting valley were covered with pines; there was also the occasional evergreen oak standing proudly tall. The upper slopes were bare and on them grew only the occasional clump of weed grass, wild thyme, rock cistus, or thistle; in parts, their nearly sheer faces had been striated by the weather so that it looked as if in some past age they had been worked by man. Along the bed of the valley there ran a torrente, normally dry, but very occasionally carrying roaring flood water.

A road ran along the west side of the valley for a couple of kilometres; then, in a succession of sharp-angled bends, wound down to the bridge which spanned the torrente. This road was unfenced throughout its length, even though at a couple of points the drop beyond was as much as thirty metres. Nervous drivers stuck nervously to the middle of the road, preferring the risk of meeting an oncoming vehicle head-on rather than approaching too close to the dangerous edge. For some years there had been a plan to erect Armco barriers at the most dangerous spots, but this had low priority since few of the millions of tourists ventured so far away from the sand and the sea.

The Ford Fiesta rounded one very sharp bend with scrabbling tyres and raced down towards the next one; its speed in such circumstances was so dangerous that it suggested either mechanical trouble or an incapacitated driver. Near the second bend, violent braking made the tyres squeal and the car entered into an incipient skid and the back wheels slid within a metre of the edge of the road, just past the apex. A driver with even a vestigial sense of self-protection would have backed right off as he sent a brief prayer of thanks to the overworked St Christopher, but the driver of the Fiesta continued at the same ridiculous speed.

The side of the mountain came out in an uneven wedge shape and the left-hander started easily, but then tightened up to become fiercer than any of the previous bends. Because of this, there was a sign denoting a dangerous corner which, since few of the others had been so marked and none of them had been less than dangerous, should have been a double warning, but it went unheeded and the Fiesta entered the bend far too fast. Only as the bend tightened right up did the driver realize the extra danger and even then his reaction was incompetent; he braked harshly. There had been a light shower a couple of hours previously and where trees overhung the road this had still not quite dried; in addition, the surface was—near the occasional oak—littered with leaves which had been blown off in the brief, but fierce, wind which had come funnelling down the valley without warning. The car skidded and this time the driver's luck did not hold. The back of the Fiesta whipped round with neck-jarring speed and slid towards and then over the edge of the road; momentum carried the car forward past the point of balance and it fell.

The rock face was almost sheer for several metres, then there was a narrow ledge on which grew a few pine trees and grass; beyond the ledge was another and much longer drop, though not quite so sheer. The car landed on the ledge, rear-end first. The force sent the front end slamming down, crunching wheels and suspension. The doors flew open and the passenger was hurled out; he tumbled into a bush, arms and legs flailing. Momentum again took the car forward. It hesitated for a second on the edge of the ledge, then went over. This time the drop was over a dozen metres, a second one even more; a final fall brought it sideways on to a huge boulder. The car was crushed into a shapeless mass of twisted metal.

The violent, screeching noise had silenced both the

cicadas and the birds, most notably a couple of crossbills, but after a while the cicadas resumed their shrilling and the birds their calling. Hot sunshine reached down to the wreck.

CHAPTER 2

Alvarez reached over to his trousers, on the chair, and extracted from the pocket a handkerchief; he wiped the sweat from his face and neck. Considering it was still only the middle of May, the heat was unusual. Or perhaps the humidity was very high. In either case, the wise man did not overwork himself.

There was a call from downstairs. 'Enrique, are you awake?'

He stared up. The sunlight was being reflected up through the louvres of the closed shutters to form a pattern on the ceiling that took his mind back to his childhood, although he couldn't pin down the exact context of the memory . . .

'Enrique. Enrique.'

'All right,' he shouted back. Dolores was an admirable woman, a fine homemaker, and a wonderful cook, but she did fuss far too much. Fussing promoted ulcers.

After a while, he sat upright and swivelled his feet round until he could put them on the floor. He yawned and looked at his watch and was surprised to discover that the time was after five. Still, there wasn't much work in hand or, at least, work which need concern him too greatly. Times might have changed and parts of Palma have become centres of mugging, but Llueso remained reasonably calm and peaceful and only the occasional tourist suffered crime; since they were seldom on the island for more than a fortnight, their cases could soon be forgotten.

He stood, pulled on his trousers and shirt; his chin tickled and he scratched it to discover that he'd forgotten to shave

that morning. He left the bedroom and went downstairs to
the kitchen. 'Where's the coffee?' he asked, as he looked
around.

Dolores said sharply: 'What's that?'

He belatedly realized that she was in one of her moods.
Admirable woman that she was, she did have them. Jaime
ought to have stopped this long ago, but he'd always been
inclined to settle for an easy life rather than an authoritative
one.

'Has the cat taken your tongue?'

'I just thought . . .'

'I know exactly what you thought. That I was here to
slave for you. Coffee is to be ready exactly when you want
it and never mind how busy I am. It is enough that you
want your coffee now!' Her oval face, framed by jet black
hair, was filled with haughty anger.

'There's no need to bother if you're too busy.'

She rested her hands on her hips. 'So now you wish to
insult me by suggesting I'd let you leave the house without
a mug of coffee and a slice of coca to last you until supper?'

'But you've just said . . .'

'Sit.'

He sat at the kitchen table. Perhaps Jaime wasn't really
so much to blame. After all, how could any husband deal
with a wife who was so illogical? He wondered if he should
have asserted himself and left? But her coca was always as
light as a fairy's footprint . . .

He arrived at the guardia building at a quarter to six and
the cabo on duty looked up from a girlie magazine and said
that Palma had repeatedly been trying to contact him by
telephone. He climbed the stairs slowly. When he reached
his office, he slumped down in the chair behind the desk
and briefly looked at the morning's mail which was as yet
unopened. He transferred his gaze to the window and the
sun-splashed wall of the house on the other side of the street.
He heard a girl singing and knew a sudden happiness that

now girls could spend their youth singing instead of working all day in the fields so that in later life they were crippled from arthritis and rheumatism.

The telephone rang. Superior Chief Salas's secretary, a woman who spoke as if her mouth were full of overripe plums, informed him that the superior chief wished to speak to him.

Salas, typically, offered no friendly greeting, but immediately demanded to know where in the devil he'd been all afternoon and then, with Madrileño vulgarity, made it clear he was unconvinced by the answer. 'Then perhaps now you could manage to find the time to concentrate on your work? . . . Early yesterday afternoon there was a fatal accident on the Estemos road; a car went off at one of the corners. One man was thrown clear and he's now in the Clínica Bahía, the other died instantly. Neither man carried any means of identification. Find out who they are.'

'But, señor, surely the survivor in the clinic can say that?'

'Doubtless he could, if only he were not suffering from amnesia.'

'Oh! . . . And he had no papers on him?'

'The fact that you need to make inquiries surely tells you that he had none?'

'What about the car?'

'It was hired and the man who handled the hiring has returned to his home in Madrid because of illness in the family and the other staff can't find any record. Typical incompetence.'

'Where was the car hired?'

'At the airport.'

'Then it's possible the two men are foreigners?'

'Why do you imagine I've asked you to handle the matter rather than someone in whom I'd have greater confidence? I told you at the beginning that the injured man speaks English, but hardly any Spanish.'

'In fact, señor, you didn't mention that.'

'I know precisely what I said. Kindly concentrate. I want a full report on my desk by tomorrow morning at the latest. Is that clear?'

'I'll do my best.'

'I was hoping for a more forceful contribution.'

'Who do I speak to about the crash?'

'Gómez, B divisional HQ.' He cut the connection.

Alvarez opened the top left-hand drawer of the desk and brought out a small booklet in which were listed the telephone numbers of all departments of the guardia civil. He found the number, rang it, spoke to Gómez.

'The crash took place at just after three, yesterday, Wednesday, according to the smashed watch on the dead man's wrist. The car was travelling eastwards on the Estemos road and had just passed kilometre post thirty-seven.'

Alvarez visualized the area, so isolated and, in parts, even harsh that it could have been a continent removed from any tourist beach.

'They tried to take the tightest bend on that road far too fast and the car went over the edge. It hit a ledge which flipped open the doors and since the passenger wasn't wearing a seat-belt he was thrown clear, but the driver was belted in and he carried on all the way down. He never stood a chance.'

'What did the passenger do—climb back up to the road and call for help?'

'He was too confused to do anything constructive. We found him just wandering around half way between the road and the wreck.'

'If he didn't call you out, who did?'

'Another car came along and the driver stopped short of the bend for a leak. He saw something in the torrente glinting in the sun, walked round the bend to find out what it was, realized the crash could only just have happened and drove on to the nearest telephone, four kilometres away.'

'Why didn't he climb down to help the passenger?'

'He'd no idea that there was one. All he saw was the wrecked car. The passenger must have been hidden by the trees.'

'Wouldn't he have heard the car stop on the road?'

'Who knows? He can't speak Spanish and anyway was knocked silly.'

'He was lucky, then, that this other car stopped.'

'Right. Still, the hospital says his injuries aren't serious and he'll get over his confusion problems. I suppose that in the end he'd have got himself up to the road if no one had stopped.'

'And you haven't been able to identify either him or the driver?'

'After we'd got the driver out—and if I told you what that was like, you'd not want any supper—we searched him and the car. No papers of any sort.'

'And the same with the passenger?'

'Right again. And the only luggage was a backpack, the kind hikers use with an aluminium frame. That contained clothes and some tinned food, but nothing else.'

'Did you try to get a name out of the passenger even though he was so confused?'

'My oppo did, since he reckons he's learned a lot of English from the birds he's pulled on the beaches. Never got anywhere. Not learning the right kind of English, maybe.'

'It's funny, neither of them having any papers.'

'Not necessarily. Last week I stopped a car for crossing a solid line in the middle of a village at twice the speed limit and the driver, who was English, said he never carried any papers around with him because he didn't have to at home. I bloody near told him to clear off back there.'

'Even so, the backpack suggests a hiker. You'd expect him to carry means of identification around . . . I gather you've been on to a car hire firm at the airport?'

'Not me.'

'Who did get in touch with them?'

'I've no idea.'

'D'you know the name?'

'Worldwide Hire Cars.' Gómez's pronunciation of the English words was so poor that Alvarez had to ask three times for them to be repeated.

He thanked Gómez and rang off, phoned the car hire firm at the airport and spoke to a woman with a voice of honey and spice.

'I'm sorry, but I just can't answer you, Inspector. It's all very worrying and I've had the manager shouting down the phone, but Toni handled that hiring and when his mother was suddenly taken ill, he flew back to Madrid.'

'But somewhere there must be the usual record of the hiring?'

'Yes, of course. But as I said to the manager, I just can't find it. You see, I'm only relieving Toni and I don't know his system of filing.'

'Have you any idea when he'll be back?'

'As a matter of fact, he phoned an hour ago to say his mother's much better and he reckons to return early tomorrow.'

'Then I'll be along to have a word with him in the morning.'

He rang off, dialled the Clínica Bahía. A nurse told him that the unnamed patient's physical injuries were relatively minor and he was making a good recovery from them, but his mind was still very confused and his loss of memory complete. The prognosis? The doctors were slightly surprised that his mind should still be so confused—he didn't seem to have suffered any heavy blows to the head—but it was always very difficult to be certain about the brain; in the circumstances, they could offer no prognosis.

He replaced the receiver and relaxed. Toni was in Madrid, the car's passenger didn't know a thing. Even Salas, then, would have to agree that there was nothing more that could be done for the moment. His thoughts wandered. Hadn't

Dolores said that she was cooking lomo con col for supper . . .

CHAPTER 3

Terminal A was in chaos; long queues had formed at several check-in points, some of which were still not manned, the departure board had not been altered since the previous evening, the arrival board was not working at all, the public address system had hysterics, and the information desk was manned by an attractive woman who was too busy flirting over the telephone to monitor the VDU in front of her, which in any case was rolling so heavily that it was impossible to read, while the luggage handlers were having their second merienda of the morning so that all carousels in the arrival lounges were empty. A typical morning at Son San Juan airport.

Alvarez threaded his way through the press of people around the outer doors of the arrival hall and crossed to the line of booths which were occupied by representatives of various car hire firms. Above one of the middle ones was the name, in blue lettering on a white background, World-wide Car Hire.

A man, who was working at the desk, looked up. He noted Alvarez's less-than-smart appearance. 'Yes?' he asked in bored tones.

'Are you Toni Bibiloni?'

'And what if I am?'

'Inspector Alvarez, Cuerpo General de Policía.'

Bibiloni stood with studied elegance. He was dressed in lilac-coloured shirt and light green linen trousers. He was tall, slim, sleekly handsome, and very self-assured. 'You've come about the car that crashed?'

'That's right.' Alvarez's reaction was as immediate as it

was irrational—he disliked the man. 'Did the hirer pay by credit card or cash?'

'Cash.'

'Why isn't there any record of the hiring?'

'There is.'

'The person I spoke to yesterday . . .'

'Dear Tania,' said Bibiloni languidly. 'A simply charming person, but so inclined to muddle. She failed to look in the right place.'

Ten to one, thought Alvarez uncharitably, there was some sort of fiddle going on; probably Bibiloni diverted cash into his own pocket. It wouldn't be difficult, provided he'd got his hands on an extra supply of forms. If there were no queries, the cash stayed with him and there was no official record of the hiring; if there was, he simply 'found' the copy of the hiring contract and the money, carefully put on one side . . .

'Is there anything more?'

Alvarez jerked his thoughts back to the present. 'I'd like to have a look at it.'

'Presumably, you're referring to the copy of the hiring agreement?' Bibiloni turned, crossed to the desk, took a key from his pocket and unlocked one of the drawers, brought out a folder from which he extracted two carbon copies, one of which he handed over.

Alvarez read. Steven Thompson. Address on the island, Hotel Verde, Cala Oraña; passport number, C 229570 A; English driving licence number, 255038 ST16KD; date of hiring, 14th to 17th May. He looked up. 'Do you remember this hiring?'

'Of course.'

'Was he on his own?'

'Yes.'

'Had he flown from Britain?'

'I can't say.'

'He didn't mention where he'd come from?'

'No. Only that it was warmer here.'

'Which makes it sound as if he had come from Britain?'

'If you say so.'

'Did he mention why he was only going to be on the island for four days?'

'No.'

'What luggage did he have?'

'A small suitcase and one of those executive briefcases.'

'Then he might have been here on business?'

'Why not?'

'Did he speak Spanish well?'

'Since I am fluent in English, that is what we spoke; it's so much easier than listening to someone mispronouncing everything.'

Alvarez returned the copy of the hiring agreement. 'Make certain this doesn't disappear again until my inquiries are completed.'

Bibiloni shrugged his shoulders, but his expression was now watchful rather than supercilious.

Alvarez left and walked out through the west doors. The sky was cloudless and the sun was hot and by the time he reached his car he was sweating. Too much alcohol, too many cigarettes, and too much food; he must remember his resolution to cut back on all three, he thought, as he unlocked the driving door and sat, then hurriedly opened his window and turned on the fan because the interior of the ancient Seat 600 was like an oven. He picked up the pack of cigarettes on the front passenger seat and lit one, remembered his decision of only minutes before, decided that it would be a terrible waste to throw the cigarette away.

He drove on the autoroute until it came to an end, then continued along the Paseo Marítimo, the wide, elegant road which ringed the bay and gave a quick route to the west side of Palma and the succession of concrete jungles which had done so much to ruin what had once been one of the most beautiful bays in the Mediterranean.

Cala Oraña had originally been a small bay with a wide, curving beach that was backed by land of such poor quality that it had supported only scrub trees and undergrowth on which a few goats and hollow-ribbed sheep had browsed. It had escaped the first wave of development which had swept the island because the land had been left to two minors who were therefore unable to sell, even thought the price then offered had been very good. Their immediate loss became their ultimate gain. By the time both had attained their majority, the land they owned was worth many times its previous value because it was now one of the very last stretches of coastline undeveloped. They'd sold to a company whose directors had had more imagination and taste, if no less greed, than most of their competitors and the company had promoted an up-market development, aimed at attracting people who wanted to live or holiday within easy reach of Palma, but who were not prepared to suffer the sardine-ugliness of a Magalluf. Only two hotels and two appartment blocks were built and none of these was more than four floors high; on the rest of the land were medium to large luxurious villas, each in a plot of at least two thousand square metres. And, as an added bonus, all sewage pipes discharged into the next bay.

Hotel Verde was on the east side of the bay. Designed by a Brazilian architect, it was sharply modernistic in appearance, yet a certain restraint had made certain that it remained just in taste for a traditionalist; even the exterior green tiling, which had provided the pedestrian name, complemented rather than exaggerated. It was surrounded on three sides by a well-tended garden and on the fourth by the sand and the sea.

Parking was to the right of the main entrance and Alvarez drew in alongside a Mercedes 190E on tourist plates. He left his car, stared at the Mercedes and then at his 600 and sighed, climbed the steps up on to the patio and went through swing doors into a large foyer, cool and comfortable.

The reception desk was manned by two men, dressed in black coats and ties. He introduced himself to the elder and explained what he wanted. The receptionist had a word with the assistant manager, then showed Alvarez into the office behind the reception desk.

The assistant manager was tall for a Mallorquin, pale-faced, suggesting he seldom went out in the sun, and clearly somewhat harassed. He picked up a pencil and fiddled with it. 'You're trying to find out something about the unfortunate Señor Thompson? I'll see if I can trace his booking.' He swivelled his chair round to face a small desk-top computer and VDU. He tapped out a command on the keyboard and a string of names and dates, in vertical order, appeared on the screen. He leaned forward slightly to read, suggesting he needed glasses. 'He stayed here on the fourteenth, just for the one night.'

'How did he book?'

He deleted that list, entered another command and a second one appeared. He frowned. 'I wish the damned thing wouldn't get so muddled up.' He cleared the screen and summoned up a third list. 'Booked by telephone. There was no confirmatory letter, but then the call was only two days prior to the booking.'

'Have you any idea where he telephoned from?'

'None.'

'Did you meet him?'

'I didn't, no. In my job, I really only meet guests if they're complaining about something and the desk can't cool them down. Which is far too often.'

'Would it be possible to have a word with whoever booked him in and also to see the register?'

The assistant manager stood and went to the doorway and called in the younger receptionist, who brought with him a large cloth-bound book. This, opened, he passed over. Alvarez read the penultimate entry. Steven Thompson, British passport number C 229570 A, registered from the

14th to the 15th. 'Haven't you had more than one other guest since he was here?' he asked curiously.

'Good heavens, yes! That's the register for the independents; we naturally keep a separate one for the packages.' His tone said far more than his words. They would have chosen to cater solely for the independent traveller, but the world had changed and now even the luxury hotels had to accept bookings from package holiday operators. But those which were staffed by persons who still appreciated the difference between quality and quantity maintained what standards they could.

Alvarez spoke to the receptionist, handing back the register as he did so. 'Do you remember Señor Thompson?'

'I'm afraid I don't really. You see, it was change-over day and there's always trouble then.'

'D'you think any of the other staff would be likely to remember him?'

The assistant manager answered. 'The porter would have carried his bags . . . Who was on duty then?'

'Servero, I think,' said the receptionist.

'See if you can find him, will you, and ask him to come in here. But before you go . . . Inspector, would you like a drink?'

'A coñac would go down very well.'

'And I'll have my usual.'

The receptionist left and there was a short wait, then the porter, dressed in traditional waistcoat, entered the office, a tray in his hand. 'I was told to bring this along in a hurry,' he said, as he put the tray down on the desk. He was in his late fifties and had learned to perfection the art of insolent servility as found in most British hotels.

The assistant manager picked up the balloon glass of brandy and leaned across to pass it to Alvarez. 'The Inspector wants to ask you a few questions,' he said, just before he drank from the glass of still orangeade.

The porter's expression became wary.

'Do you remember Señor Thompson?' Alvarez said. 'He was here Monday night.'

'He was an independent,' said the assistant manager.

'Ah! You must be talking about the gentleman who arrived in a white Ford Fiesta.'

'He certainly was in a Fiesta,' said Alvarez, 'but I can't say what the colour was.'

'And his luggage was one small suitcase and a director's case.'

'That's right.'

'I've a very good memory,' said the porter complacently, apparently forgetting that initially he had appeared to be having difficulty in recalling the guest. 'Beautiful quality luggage. Not like most of them who come here; plastic for them.'

'You carried his luggage in?'

'That's right.'

'Will you tell me exactly what happened from the moment you met him?'

The porter, intent on proving just how excellent his memory really was, spoke at length. He'd carried the luggage in and across to the desk. The señor, allocated Room 34, had registered. He'd taken the key and had led the way up to the third floor and along the right-hand corridor to the end room. He'd unlocked the door and ushered the señor inside. He'd casually remarked that this was the nicest room in the hotel. It always made a guest feel doubly welcome to be singled out for special attention; or to think he had been.

'Was he talkative?'

'Very friendly, not like some of the people we get here.'

'Did you speak in Spanish or English?'

'English.'

'What did he talk about?'

'This and that. I asked him if he'd been to the island before.'

'Had he?'

'Several times . . . D'you mind telling me a bit more of what this is all about? I mean, he was a real gent—you can't mistake 'em, not if you've been in the job as long as I have—so what's the problem?'

'Unfortunately, he's been killed in a car crash and although we now know his name, we can't find any reference that will enable us to contact his next-of-kin.'

'There must be something written down in his papers.'

'We don't know for certain he was carrying any,' said Alvarez patiently.

'Then what d'you think was in his director's case?'

'We don't know because we haven't found it.'

'Then what about his wallet?'

'That was also missing . . . Did he comment on any of his previous visits? Did he suggest when they were or where he stayed?'

'Nothing like that.'

'D'you reckon he was deliberately avoiding any definite references?'

The porter, sharp but not particularly intelligent, was bewildered by the question and it had to be repeated in a different form before he answered: 'I wouldn't have said he was.'

'You learned nothing about his life?'

The porter scratched his neck. 'Only how much he liked sailing.'

'How d'you know that?'

'Because he talked about it and said as how it had been too squally for the past few days to take his boat out.'

'He talked about "his" boat?'

'That's what I've just said.'

'Anything more?'

'No.'

'If you should remember anything, get in touch, will you?'

'I've told you everything; I've a good memory.'

'Then thanks for all your help.'

The porter went over to the door, opened it, turned. 'I'll tell you one thing. He was a real gentleman.' He went out.

The assistant manager spoke drily. 'Obviously, the señor tipped him generously.'

Alvarez looked at his empty glass and wondered if the hotel would prove equally generous.

CHAPTER 4

Clínica Bahía, the smallest of the state hospitals in Palma, was situated on the eastern boundary of the city. It was an ugly slab of a building and inside little attempt had been made to brighten its image so that the gloomy reception area correctly set the scene. Plans either to replace or to modernize it were regularly updated, but never exercised. Yet despite this, the staff were efficient and cheerful and they usually managed to uplift a patient's morale.

Alvarez took the lift to the fourth floor and then walked along the right-hand corridor to the small recess in which was a desk for the nursing staff and, on either side of this, wash- and store-rooms. A young nurse was working at some papers and he explained what he wanted.

'Señor Higham? He's in Room 413.'

He spoke with sharp surprise. 'Then you have managed to find out his name?'

'I didn't because I don't speak any English and his Spanish sounds like Portuguese.' She grinned. 'But Dr Bauzá did post-graduate work in America and so he can speak English; he discovered the señor had recovered his memory.'

'Has it fully returned?'

'I couldn't say exactly, but I think it must have done because Dr Bauzá said he's making a good recovery and ought to be able to leave quite soon.'

'That's good . . . All right if I have a chat with him?'

'I don't see why not. But if he starts looking tired, you'll have to stop immediately.'

Most of the rooms on the floor contained four beds, but 413 had only two and the second one was empty. Higham was sitting up reading a paperback. A man in his middle forties, he had a round, plump face. A small, neat moustache, the same light brown as his hair, was set above a wide, cheerful mouth. The only visible signs that he had been in a car accident were the plaster on his right cheek and a bruise which stretched across his right chin.

Alvarez introduced himself, then said how delighted he was to find the other better.

'No more delighted than I am, I can assure you!' His voice was warm and tuneful. 'These last few days have been like . . . The nearest I can get to it is, it's been like having a spider's web throttling my brain. I've kept struggling to get my thoughts lined up straight, but they just wouldn't. Been rather frightening, really; a bit of me could still think and keep wondering if I'd gone round the twist. But, thank God, that's all over and done with and now I can think as straight as I ever could, which maybe isn't as straight as it ought to be . . .' He laughed, then became serious. 'Look, maybe you can tell me something. How's the other man, the driver? No one here seems to know. I've got this very hazy idea that he must have been badly hurt . . .'

'I am afraid that he died in the crash.'

'My God!' He fiddled with his moustache as he stared into the distance. 'I didn't realize things were that bad . . . I was lucky, then?'

'Very lucky. And almost certainly because you were not wearing your seat-belt so that you were thrown clear.'

'You never know, do you? Wear a belt and save your life; don't wear it and save your life.'

'Do you feel strong enough to answer a few questions?'

'I'm fine.'

Alvarez settled on the spare bed. 'We've had a bit of a problem because until this morning no one knew who either you or the driver was.'

'I don't follow. I mean, I wasn't sparking on all four cylinders, I know, but you've got my passport. And Steve must have had papers on him.'

'There were no papers of any sort on either of you.'

'But there must have been.'

'I'm afraid not. Where was your passport?'

'Everything like that was in my backpack. It was far too hot to wear a coat and papers and money aren't safe in a trouser pocket . . . You're not saying my money's gone as well?'

'We didn't find any.'

'You looked in the backpack?'

'It was thoroughly searched.'

'Christ! That just caps everything.'

'Was your money in cash?'

'Not very much. Most of it was in travellers' cheques . . . Then I did hear someone and it wasn't imagination!'

'How d'you mean?'

Higham shook his head, as if to clear it; he spoke quickly. 'The worst part was seeing what was going to happen and not being able to stop it. I tried to grab the wheel and steer us away, but it was no good. As we went over, I can remember thinking: So this is what it's like to crash. And then things got painful. And now they're still confused even though everything else is back to normal. I'm pretty certain I shouted for help for a while; nothing happened, so I picked myself up and stumbled around, but I kept falling over things . . . And it was when I was lying on the ground, too weak to move any more, that I thought I heard voices. I called out, but they didn't seem to hear me and in the end I kind of decided that the voices had only been in my mind. But if the money's gone, there probably was someone, wasn't there?'

'It certainly seems so,' he agreed, angered that there could
be men who'd rob the dead and the injured and leave the
injured to his fate. 'Do you have any idea whether Señor
Thompson had much money on him?'

'He must have had a fair bit. After all, he gave me lunch
at a restaurant that certainly wasn't cheap and there was
still plenty left in his wallet when he'd finished paying.'

'Would you like to guess how much?'

'I wouldn't. I mean, I took care not to take too much
interest.'

'Of course . . . You heard talking, which means two or
more men. Did you understand anything they said or did
the rhythm of their speech suggest what language they were
talking?'

'No to both. Like I said, it was all so hazy I wasn't even
certain I really was hearing 'em.'

'Señor, have you been long on the island?'

'Hardly any time at all. You see, I didn't leave England
until . . .'

His job in England, a wages clerk, had been boring but
safe. He'd married a little later than his pals, after he'd
saved quite a bit of money—he'd always led a steady life
although ever since he'd been a youngster he'd dreamed of
adventure. Debbie had been considerably younger than he.
At first, that hadn't mattered. Probably it never would have
done if her sister hadn't married a man who knew all the
dodges, especially how to work the more profitable VAT
fiddles. Spent money like water. Debbie's sister had flaunted
new clothes, jewellery, cars . . . Debbie had become as sour
as hell and had nagged and nagged him to find another job
where he'd make better money. Against his will, he'd moved.
Things had worked out OK for a while, even though his
income still fell far short of his brother-in-law's—but then
cheap imports from the Far East had hit his new firm so
hard that it had very nearly been bankrupted. Inevitably,
there'd been redundancies and these had been based on

the usual last in, first out. His redundancy money hadn't strained its brown envelope . . .

He'd hoped Debbie would understand; after all, if he hadn't moved, he'd still have a job. But she hadn't been willing to understand anything or to stand by him and she'd cleared out. Soon afterwards, he'd heard that she'd moved in with a friend of her brother-in-law who ran a Porsche and thought that a twenty-pound note was loose change.

Strangely, despite the bitter pain, his overriding emotion had been one of anger, directed not at her or her lover, but at himself. Why had he been such a bloody fool as to allow himself to be so trapped by conformity—since sixteen, all dreams ignored and all ambition directed towards a steady job with a pension, a house on mortgage, a worthwhile savings account—that he'd laid himself open to such hurt? And in his anger, he'd sworn an ending to all conformity. Draw a line through his past life and start again. Remember those dreams. Wander the world . . .

He'd sold the house and paid off the mortgage. He'd left that road in which he'd lived all those dead years without saying goodbye to anyone. He'd drifted through France, crossed the Pyrenees, taken months on the journey down to Valencia, where he'd spent the winter in the company of other, mostly much younger, drifters. In March, his feet had begun to itch once more. Someone had talked about standing on the north-west coast of Mallorca and watching the sun sink below the sea and discovering one's immortal soul. He didn't give a damn about his soul, but the mental image had triggered a desire. He'd crossed in the ferry, hitch-hiked to somewhere with a name like Son Ella, and had stood on a high cliff and watched the blood-red, oblate sun sink below the sea. It had been slightly eerie. No wonder ancient man had been scared at every sunset that the sun wouldn't reappear . . . 'I'm sorry. God knows why I'm going on and on like this. You probably won't believe me, but usually I don't bore other people with my problems.'

'Señor, I have not been bored. And perhaps it's good for you to speak about all these things.'

'Yes, but . . .' He stopped.

Alvarez smiled. 'But being an Englishman, you do not like to put your emotions on display?'

Higham looked embarrassed.

'Tell me, how did you come to meet Señor Thompson?'

'I was walking along the road, hot and tired, trying to thumb a lift. He stopped and when he heard I'd no definite objective, said he'd show me a part of the island tourists didn't usually see. We drove up into the mountains.'

'Then he knew the island well; perhaps had a house here?'

'He knew it well, yes. But from something he said, I'm pretty certain he didn't own any property here.'

'Did he mention friends and where they live?'

'No, he didn't. In fact, looking back, I'd say he was one of those types who's always interested in other people, but is careful never to talk about himself much.'

'I think he gave you lunch?'

'We stopped at a restaurant right up in the mountains that had a fantastic view. The place was obviously pretty pricey and I told him I just couldn't afford it. He said the meal was to be on him. Frankly, that had me thinking just for a second.'

'Thinking what?'

'Whether he was a queer and had me in his sights.'

'Do you think that was right?'

'No way. He was just one of those blokes who likes meeting people and hearing about them.'

'Did he drink a lot?'

'No. He mentioned that since early morning he'd had a migraine threatening and booze was one of the things which could bring on an attack. But that didn't stop him giving me a couple of drinks before the meal and ordering a good bottle of wine; so by the end, I was very cheerful, thank you . . .

'We hadn't long left the restaurant when he stopped the car. He was sick; God, how he was sick! When he'd begun to recover, I offered to drive, but he said the car was only insured for him and in any case he was OK. So he started up again. And then . . . He had another attack, much worse than the first and didn't stop in time. We started weaving all over the road and going like the clappers. I tried to grab the wheel, but he'd still got hold of it . . . And that's how we went over the edge.'

'A very frightening experience. Thank you, señor, for telling me.' Alvarez stood.

'D'you have to go, then?'

'Yes, I do.'

'D'you think . . . Is there any chance you could drop in again some time and have another chat? I mean, with no one but the doctor speaking English, I'm cut right off.'

'I certainly will call in if I can.'

'That's great. And if you do, I don't know if there'd be any chance of finding an English newspaper?'

'I will try.'

'That's a real pal . . . Just one more thing. D'you think there's much hope of recovering my cash?'

'Frankly, I'm afraid not.'

'If I could get my hands on those bastards . . . Still, at least I'll get a refund on the travellers' cheques.'

'Perhaps I can help you over that. Sometimes in order to claim one needs a note from the police to confirm that the loss has been reported to them.'

'That's a thought. D'you think you could let me have something?'

'Indeed.'

'Then thanks again.'

Alvarez said goodbye and left. On the ground floor there was a newsagent and in this he found a copy of the *Daily Mail*. He bought it, took the lift back up to the fourth floor and handed the paper to a nurse and asked her to give it to

Higham. Then he returned downstairs and left the building. He was glad to escape. He loathed hospitals because they reminded him that he was only mortal.

CHAPTER 5

After a slightly delayed siesta—since he'd returned late from Palma—and a subsequent and essential cup of coffee, Alvarez left the kitchen and went through to the front room and the telephone. He reported to the superior chief.

'You've hardly made any progress,' complained Salas.

'On the contrary, señor,' he began, somewhat piqued, 'I've identified both men and determined the cause of the accident . . .'

'Have you discovered who's the dead man's nearest relative and where he or she lives?'

'No . . .'

'Or the name and address of any friend who lives on the island?'

'No . . .'

'Then you've attained little of any significance. Has it occurred to you to send the number of the dead man's passport to England to ask their help in tracing his next-of-kin?'

'There hasn't been time, señor. I've only just returned from making my inquiries. But it's my intention to get on to England the moment I ring off now . . .'

'Inspector, if you could contrive actually to accomplish one quarter of what you're always about to do, your crime figures would be impressive instead of a disgrace.'

'Señor, my clear-up rate is quite good . . .'

'Only because you carefully forget to record, let alone investigate, a large proportion of the crimes committed,' snapped Salas, before he cut the connection.

Alvarez replaced the receiver. Sadly, Salas lacked the right attitude to command; praise, for him, was a dirty word. He returned to the dining-room, went over to the large sideboard, and opened the right-hand cupboard.

'What are you looking for?' demanded Dolores, startling him.

He looked at her as she stood in the doorway of the kitchen. 'I was just wondering if there was coñac for after the meal or whether I needed to go out to buy some.'

'There's half a bottle, which is far more than you two are going to drink this evening,' she said aggressively.

He wondered if he should go ahead and pour himself a drink now, which had been his original intention, quickly decided that that would hardly be politic since she was obviously in one of her more belligerent moods. 'That's all right, then.' He closed the cupboard door.

'You would be much healthier if you stopped drinking.'

'Yes, I suppose I might be.'

She glared at him, returned into the kitchen. A moment later, there was the ringing noise of something dropping on to the floor, followed by an angry expression of such vulgarity that he hastily assured himself he must have mistaken the words.

He looked at the clock. An hour before the meal. Just time, then, to go along to the guardia post and his office, there to phone through the details of the passport so that inquiries could be made in England. He stood. What right had Salas to imply that he did not show a keen initiative?

The next morning, Alvarez was preparing to leave the house —a little on the late side because he had slept through two calls from Dolores—when the undertaker from Fogufol rang. 'I've been on to Palma and they told me to talk to you because you're in charge.'

'In charge of what?'

'The car crash, of course. What am I to do with the stiff? Is there to be a funeral or isn't there?'

'Of course there is,' he replied testily. 'But until we can trace the next-of-kin, we don't know whether it's to be here or in England.'

'Are you saying I'm to keep him in store until I hear from you?'

'I'm saying exactly that.'

'You realize it's costing?'

'You'll be paid.'

'Just you remember that from now on you're responsible for seeing that it is.'

Alvarez replaced the receiver. No one could be prouder of being a Mallorquin than he, but that pride didn't blind him to the fact that for many of his countrymen money had become the most important part of life—or death.

In Palma, the litter-boxes and bins were emptied six times a week in late spring, summer, and early autumn, since in the heat anything perishable rotted very quickly. As the dustman lifted out the inner wire basket of one of the lamp-post boxes in Calle Arnoux, he saw among the paper and orange peel a wallet, between the two halves of which was a blue passport. He opened the passport. It belonged to Jack Higham.

Muriel Taylor looked at her reflection in the dressing-table mirror and initially was well satisfied, but then she noticed the curl of hair on the right-hand side. That blasted woman, she thought. The best hair salon in Palma and the head assistant couldn't trim properly. Archie had recently remarked that the country ran in spite of the people who worked in it, not because of them. He originally must have heard someone else say that.

She examined her face again. No one would ever guess from her appearance that she was closing up fast on forty.

Her skin had the purity and tautness of a twenty-year-old. Her eyes were an unusual blue; men were fascinated by them. Her nose was Grecian. A friend had once called her mouth Roman patrician. Truly cosmopolitan. Her teeth were white and regular and an advertisement for her dentist in Harley Street; she couldn't understand why so many of the British risked going to the local dentists who, for all she knew, still worked with treadle drills.

She left the stool and stood so that she could see herself in the full-length mirror. She had a near-perfect figure, hardly thickening anywhere, thanks to a rigorous diet, exercise, and will-power. She crossed to the longest of the built-in cupboards and slid back the right-hand door. Which dress to wear? Not too smart or it would be completely out of place. She chose a print frock which she had bought in Palma on a day when she was feeling dismal and needed to do something to buck herself up. She hadn't worn it again because once she'd cheered up she'd rightly decided it lacked chic, but today that would be an advantage. 'Oh, God, what a bloody bore!' she said aloud, thinking of the luncheon and all the pleased-to-meet-you women to whom she'd have to make the effort to be polite.

Not that she was a snob. Very far from it. She believed in valuing a person for himself, not because of his background. Not, of course, that that meant that she was indifferent to those backgrounds. She rightly demanded standards, even if she was broad-minded about them. She didn't hold that wealth was an essential. She knew one or two people whose incomes were as low as £25,000 a year yet who were perfectly pleasant. Schooling was important, but not an immutable criterion. Certainly the public schools —that was, Eton, Harrow, and Winchester—produced gentlemen, but the products of the bourgeois places, such as Sherborne, could often pass for same . . .

She slid the frock over her head and wriggled herself into it, zipped up the side, smoothed down the front, re-examined herself in the mirror. On her, since she added considerable *ton*, the frock wasn't nearly as *déclassé* as on the hanger. But it would still suit its purpose because the other women wouldn't be able to take offence. It was very important not to shame them and thus incur their strange envies. The Surbiton golf club secretary's wife, Archie had called them. That also had to be a remark he had heard someone else make . . .

She took off the dress and hung it up, put on the print frock she had been wearing before. A neat little Cardin number which suited her to perfection.

She left the bedroom and went down the wide, curving staircase into the large hall. Many of the houses in the area were little boxes, built for and by people without either money or taste, but Ca'n Grande had been designed for an Armenian, and one could say what one liked about Armenians, the few educated ones had good taste and a developed, if at times oily, sense of beauty. Archie said that Ca'n Grande was like a spinnaker in a light breeze. She rather liked the analogy, even though it was too fanciful to be in really good taste. He was an amusing and comfortable companion to have around the place, offering the same devoted companionship as a bob-tailed sheepdog, but without all the mess of cast hairs. Of course, he wasn't particularly intelligent—which sometimes made her wonder why he had not risen higher in the Navy—but he was properly mannered. It was a pity that his elder brother had inherited both title and estate.

One of the maids came into the hall. 'Good morning, señora,' she said in broken English.

'Good morning, Catalina.' Muriel did not speak Spanish. She was not the kind of person to go native.

'You wish breakfast?'

She nodded. When she'd bought the house and had agreed to continue to employ the staff, she had encountered in them a regrettable tendency towards familiarity, Mallorquins having strange notions about equality. But she had soon taught them to show her due respect.

She went into the breakfast-room. The house was built on an outcrop of rock and the breakfast-room was to the south-east so that beyond the window was the patio and then, below, the sea. Few other homes on the island could boast so magnificent a view.

Catalina entered, carrying a tray. She carefully placed on the small circular table a silver teapot, milk jug, saccharine dispenser, toast rack with two slices of carefully triangulated toast, small bowl of Cooper's marmalade, and a large bowl containing oranges, tangerines, and very large white grapes.

'Thank you, Catalina.' She was invariably polite to her servants, even though she paid them. Only a parvenu was rude to staff.

She sat, spread the clean table napkin over her lap— serviette was for those who were ignorant or snobbishly unaware that napkin had by far the superior pedigree, being descended from Middle English—and helped herself to a piece of toast and marmalade. There was no butter. She had given up butter at breakfast because of the starving hordes in Africa.

She heard a car, looked at her watch and realized that this couldn't be Archie because she'd ordered him never to arrive before eleven o'clock. Then the car would be continuing on to the house which stood to the left of, and well below, Ca'n Grande. A Greek lived there. Greece might have joined the Common Market and he might be as rich as Crœsus, but she had nothing to do with him because he always belched after eating. She finished the first piece of toast, poured herself out some tea. She must make certain that Archie sat between her and the chairwoman at the luncheon. The chairwoman was a large, stout, and very earnest woman, filled with good works, whose husband had been something like a butcher. Archie was wonderful at dealing with butchers' widows. In fact, he was rather a dear.

If only he had some money, it would have been amusing to be married to him for a while . . . Good God! she thought, astounded. Hadn't her last marriage taught her anything? She finished her breakfast, furious because she had reminded herself of all the humiliation she had for years been so determined to forget.

She pressed the bell to tell Catalina to clear the table, opened the French window and stepped out on to the patio which ran round three sides of the house. The slightest of breezes ruffled the curls on her head as it brought the tang of the sea. She crossed to the swing seat, with wide overhead awning, and sat. A slight suntan was chic, a heavy one antipodean. In any case, too much sun stripped out the natural oils and replaced them with years. Several of her friends looked very much older than she.

There was the sound of another car approaching and this time it turned into the drive. If this was Archie, the time was eleven o'clock. There were moments when she wondered about his strict regard for time; was there, hidden away in his family tree, a rather serious mésalliance?

Catalina stepped out on to the patio. 'Señora, is Señor Wheeldon.'

'Tell him I am at home.'

Archibald Devreux Peregrine Wheeldon was large, cheerful, and boyishly handsome; the tight, curly hair which topped his oval face had been handed on through at least ten generations. His nose had been broken in a school boxing match and had not been properly set, the triangular scar to the right of his mouth marked where another 'gentleman' had kicked him in an inter-house rugger match. The two blemishes prevented his handsomeness being at all feminine. In deference to Muriel's wishes that he should dress decently and not like the average expatriate, he wore a silk shirt and square and a pair of fawn linen trousers with knife-edge creases.

'Good morning, Muriel.' He leaned over and kissed her

on the cheek, knowing better than to kiss her on the lips when they were in a situation where one of the servants might see them. 'You're looking lovelier than ever.'

He was not, she thought regretfully, an original lover, but he was sincere, which was a compensation.

He looked round for a chair and picked up one of the wrought-iron ones set about a very ornate wrought-iron table.

'You can't sit on that, Archie, it's far too uncomfortable: that's for people I don't want hanging about the place. Call Catalina and tell her to bring out one of the comfortable ones.'

'It's not worth bothering her . . .'

'She's paid to be bothered. In any case, she should have had the sense to put it out before you came.'

He went over to the small speaking grille on the wall of the house, pressed the call button, and spoke in fluent Spanish.

As he returned, Muriel said: 'Have you seen Genevieve since Saturday?'

'I don't think I have.'

'Tony says that she and Henry have had a row and he's gone back to England. I wonder if that's true.'

'I shouldn't think so.'

'She has seen rather a lot of Mark recently. Why, I can't imagine. Mark's so very swarthy.'

'His mother was Italian.'

'I would presume that she came from a long way south of Italy.'

'Wherever, he's a nice enough chap.'

'Archie, you're in one of your difficult moods.'

'No, I'm not.'

'Yes, you are. You're doing nothing but argue.'

Catalina came out of the house with an aluminium-framed patio chair which she found difficulty in carrying, because of its size and shape. He hurried over and took it from her;

she thanked him, smiled, returned to the house.

He set the chair down in front of the swing seat.

'What was she saying?' asked Muriel.

'That she hoped it would take my weight.'

'How dare she be so insolent!'

'Steady on, she was only joking.'

'My servants do not joke with my guests.'

'What do you mean, guest?'

'How else do you suggest I refer to you?'

'Forget it,' he said, with sudden, sad bitterness.

She said fretfully: 'You're not going to start that again, I hope. Not today of all days.'

'What's so special about today?'

'Have you forgotten? I've got to go to that beastly luncheon—you're coming with me—and be polite to all the people I normally take such trouble to avoid.'

'Some of them are very nice. You'd like them if you'd give yourself the chance.'

'That is very cruel of you.'

'Cruel?'

'Very, very cruel. What on earth has happened to upset you so terribly?'

'Nothing has.'

'Don't be ridiculous. You're being horribly prickly and that always means something has happened. Now, what is the matter?'

'It's just something I read in the *Bulletin*.'

'If you will not stick to *The Times* . . . What have you read?'

'They've identified the man who died in the car crash up in the mountains last Wednesday.'

'Why should that matter? Surely it's not anyone we know?'

'Steven Thompson.'

'Christ!'

He was surprised by her violent reaction.

'I need a drink.'

He opened his mouth to speak.

'And if you're going to start talking about the bloody yardarm, shut up.'

'I wasn't going to. I wanted to say that I didn't think you liked him or I wouldn't have told you so starkly.'

'God, you can be a bloody fool!'

He stared out to sea, an expression of bitterness furrowing his face. He couldn't think why she was so perturbed by the news; he only knew that he had cause enough.

CHAPTER 6

Robert Reading-Smith had been born plain Smith; he'd added the Reading when he'd made his first million. His father had been imprisoned in Reading jail.

He turned over on the bed and smacked the bare bottom of the woman by his side. 'Come on, move. You'll never get rich lying in bed all morning.'

'Suppose I don't want to?' she asked in a muffled voice.

'Then you're a fool.'

She rolled over on to her side. She was a natural blonde —normally this would not have been self-evident—and she had the soft, regular, svelte beauty made familiar by Hollywood.

He prodded her.

'That hurt!'

'You loved it.'

'I think you're a bit of a bastard.'

'So my mother told me.'

She giggled. Then wondered if she ought not to have done in case he had been telling the truth under the guise of a joke. She'd known him for six days, yet still couldn't begin to keep pace with him. He could be laughing and smiling one moment, coldly vicious the next, with no discernible reason for the change.

He rolled off the bed, crossed to the nearest window, unclipped the shutters and in turn swung them open and back until they were held by the wall catches. Sunshine flooded in.

She stared at the long scar just above his right hip. It was ridiculous, but that scar had come to mean so much. A person of tactless curiosity, the first time she'd seen it she'd asked him how it had happened. He'd answered with a long and involved story which he patently had not expected her to believe. Unable to take the hint, she'd asked again, that night. The second story had been no less lengthy or involved, but it had been totally different. Why was he so secretive about the scar's true origin? Over the next few days, she had allowed that scar to become both a symbol and an indicator. If he continued to conceal the truth, their relationship would be, for him, no more than passing; if he told her the truth, their relationship would have come to mean as much to him as to her . . . In eight days, her holiday ended. The flight back to cloud and rain, the dreary street in east Hounslow, the grotty semi, her dad forever rowing with her mum, her sister acting like a tart . . . 'Where did you get that scar?'

He turned and stared at her in a way that almost frightened her. 'A knife.'

'What d'you mean, a knife?' It was going to be another ridiculous story.

'Two heavies with knives tried to turn me into a soprano, one of 'em nearly succeeded.'

'But why?'

'I'd been smarter than them.'

She realized that this might, at last, be the truth. But she still couldn't be certain. Very wealthy people didn't usually get into that sort of trouble. Or had he been in some high-powered racket? That wasn't such an absurd thought.

He was smooth, but there was no missing the inner toughness. So had he finally told her the truth? Was she going to
be able to miss that plane? Would she never again have to
see 34, Grassington Crescent . . .

'We'll spend the day on the boat,' he said. He walked
past the bed and went through to the bathroom.

They'd been out on the motor-cruiser three times already.
Each time, she'd seen the envy on the faces of the people
who'd watched them sail. God, if only she could be certain
she'd see that envy week after week . . .

In the bathroom, he stood in the shower cabinet beyond
the marble-surrounded bath and enjoyed the tingling force
of the cold water. When he'd been young, he'd bathed in a
tin tub in front of the kitchen range; very D. H. Lawrence.
It was a memory which chuckled in his mind every time
one of the women ceased to be overawed by her surroundings
and began to visualize herself as mistress of them. Silly
bitches. Hadn't they learned that life was never so generous?

He turned off the shower, slid back the curtain, and
reached for a towel. They'd sail to Cala Noña, anchor, and
drink champagne. Cala Noña could only be reached by boat
and so was not besieged by hordes of tourists.

He returned to the bedroom. She was lying in a provocative pose, but he ignored her, crossed to one of the built-in
cupboards and brought out a clean shirt, pants, and trousers.

'Are you reckoning on spending all day in bed?' he asked,
as he pulled the shirt over his shoulders.

'What's the rush?'

'I told you, you'll never get rich lying in bed.' He pulled
on his pants, then his trousers.

'Come and kiss me.'

He left the bedroom and went out on to the landing. Casa
Resta was far larger than he needed—five bedrooms, each
with an en-suite bathroom, two with dressing-rooms—but
that was one reason why he'd bought it. It was obviously a
rich man's house. He crossed to the stairs and went down

and through to the kitchen. Rosa was emptying the washing-up machine. 'Is it OK for breakfast?' he asked, in a jumbled mixture of English and Spanish.

'Yes, señor. I bought some ensaimadas on my way here.'

'That's great. We'll be going out on the boat, so will you prepare a picnic lunch?'

He admired Rosa. She'd lived a hard life, but never moaned about it and was always smiling. And if she had any thoughts about the endless stream of women who warmed his bed, she kept them to herself and always showed respect to his current companion.

He left the kitchen, crossed the hall, entered the large sitting-room and went out on to the patio. The urbanización stretched up the lower slopes of a hill some six kilometres back from the sea and his house was at the highest level. Because of the steep slope, beyond the edge of the patio there was a sheer drop of five metres. The sea was clearly visible.

He sat at the bamboo and glass table, the sun hot on the left-hand side of his face. Many years ago, when schoolmasters had still freely turned to the cane, he'd received a thrashing for failing to learn a piece of poetry; ironically, he could still remember the lines which, when it had been important, he'd forgotten. 'I am monarch of all I survey . . .' That was how he felt on his patio, looking out over the other and smaller houses of the urbanización to the distant sea.

Rosa came out of the house, a tray in her hands. 'Is the señorita not ready?'

'She won't be long.'

'I will make some fresh coffee when she arrives.'

'Don't bother. She'll have it as she finds it.'

Rosa put the tray down and set everything out. Finally, she handed him a copy of the *Majorca Daily Bulletin*.

He pulled off a piece of one of the ensaimadas, buttered it, added jam, and ate. He read the headlines and leading article on the front page. More financial troubles back home, with the pound in retreat, the balance of payments adverse, and the gold and dollar reserves dropping. None of that affected him. He wasn't a fool, so he'd moved all his money out of Britain. He turned the page. He skimmed through several small items of news, came to an article headed 'Mystery victim identified'. The man killed in the crash on Wednesday afternoon was now known to have been Steven Thompson, an Englishman.

As Pat, dressed in cotton frock because he didn't like women dressed in jeans, stepped out on to the patio, she was shocked by his expression of fierce anger.

David Swinnerton had been a highly emotional, very shy man, who'd suffered from asthma from the age of five. The asthma had so interrupted his education that by the time he was eighteen he had possessed no paper qualifications and lacking these it had been very difficult to find a job, even at a time of relatively full employment; in the end, he'd worked in a local estate agent. Being an honest man, he'd disliked the work and had been thankful when one of the partners had suggested that perhaps, in view of his frequent illness, it would be best if he sought a less stressful occupation. He had immediately agreed and left. Thereafter, he'd stayed at home, writing poetry and keeping his widowed mother company.

His mother had died some years later, as the wind screamed up the valley and buffeted the slate-roofed house as if to demolish it into a funeral pyre. That night, he had written a memorial ode which for years afterwards had had the power to bring tears to his eyes.

Despite the very high level of death duties, he'd still inherited enough from his mother not to need to have to work. Six months later, he'd married. His few friends and acquaintances had, among themselves, expressed considerable surprise that he should ever have contemplated such a step, especially with Valerie Pope. She had no claims to beauty, was completely careless about appearances, and had firm opinions on most things which she seldom hesitated to express. What all of them had failed to understand was that he needed support as well as love and she needed to support as well as to love.

After several years of marriage, spent in the isolated farmhouse to the east of Snowdon, his asthma had suddenly worsened. He'd seen several specialists, the last of whom had put the situation very bluntly; if he wished to go on living, he must move to a better climate.

He and Valerie had consulted maps and read books, then applied for an extra allowance of foreign currency on medical grounds—it was one of those periods when the British were being denied the liberty of spending their own money abroad —and when this was reluctantly granted, they'd set off for the Mediterranean coast of Spain, the south of France being too expensive.

In Barcelona they'd met an Irishman—a bit of a rogue, but amusing—who'd told them that Nirvana was an island called Mallorca. They'd sailed there on the ferry. They'd arrived on an island which was not yet tainted by tourism, except in a few places, and where there was beauty around every corner. But not the solitude he needed. No matter how deserted a coast might appear to be, or how isolated a house among the almond trees, a closer examination would disclose other houses nearby and even a short acquaintance had shown that the Mallorquins were a gregarious people who believed everyone else to be the same. (Had he foreseen what would overtake so many of these beautiful coastlines he had admired, but regretfully discarded because of nearby houses, he would have fled the island.) So he'd turned his eyes to the mountains and in an old and incredibly decrepit Fiat, in parts literally held together with string, they'd climbed up into that harsh, often threatening world so alien to the soft, cultivated plains below.

They'd found the old house completely by chance. They'd

stopped for a picnic and had decided to have a short walk afterwards, looking at the wild flowers, and during this they'd suddenly come in sight of the house half way up a slope (shades of that home in Wales), little more than a ruin, backed by terraces whose walls were crumbling and whose land was neglected.

It had taken them two days to identify the owner and when they'd asked him how much he wanted for it, he'd stared at them in perplexity. Of what possible use was this abandoned, isolated place to two foreigners? No matter. He'd named a price that was, to him, astronomical. Translated into pounds, the sum had been so little that Swinnerton had immediately agreed. In the eyes of the owner, this had confirmed the fact that all foreigners were simple-minded.

Their currency allowance did not permit the purchase of a house, as cheap as that was, so Swinnerton had done something which had amazed him even as he did it, since never before had he knowingly and willingly broken the law. He'd returned to the UK, drawn fifteen hundred pounds in cash, stowed the banknotes in his suitcase, and told the hard-faced official at the airport that the only currency he was taking out of the country was the legal twenty-five pounds.

It had taken them six months to have the house rebuilt. The workers had come from Estruig, a village at the foot of the mountains, travelling to and fro in a vehicle that was half motorbike and half car. He'd paid them four pesetas an hour and they'd eaten lunch—a hunk of bread coated with olive oil and air-dried tomatoes—in their own time. They'd often sung as they'd worked, sad, wailing songs whose Moorish ancestry was unmistakable. They'd chatted to the Swinnertons in a jumbled mixture of Spanish and Mallorquin and laughed uproariously, but without the slightest meanness, when there'd been obvious misunderstandings. For the first time he could remember, he had not been frightened by people whom he did not know well.

When the house had been finished, the well had been deepened. The foreman had said that the señor was lucky, it was a good, sweet well that would flow all the year round so that he would never be short of water. Coming from the Welsh mountains, it had never occurred to either of them that they might be. After the well had been lined with sandstone blocks, and the manual pump installed and tested, the men had repaired the walls of the terracing. When he'd asked, somewhat diffidently as he remembered conditions back home, if they'd mind very much clearing the land at the same time, they had not replied that they were builders, not gardeners, but had willingly cleared the land. Then the Swinnertons had found two men willing to work as gardeners, also paid four pesetas an hour, and in a very short time the terraces had become filled with colour.

There had been no electricity and the distribution of bottled gas had not yet become commonplace, so she had had to learn to cook on a charcoal stove and the lights had worked on poor quality paraffin. In the winter, which could be cold at that altitude, with snow lying for several days, they would have a log fire in the sitting-room and a brasero under the dining-room table to roast their legs while leaving their upper halves to chill.

Very happy, he'd written a great deal of poetry. At first, he'd tried to get his work published, but his style was emotional, his themes simple and understandable, and his construction traditional, so that it was considered pedestrian and only the occasional short poem was accepted by a magazine which needed fillers. Soon, he'd ceased to bother to send out his work. After all, every single piece was a love poem addressed to Valerie and it was only her appreciation that mattered.

They occasionally heard that the outside world was changing, but thought that this didn't concern them. Perhaps the cost of some things was rising from time to time, but their needs were simple . . .

The tourist industry expanded and prosperity flooded the island. Wages rose. Peasants who had eaten meat only during the winter when a pig was killed, now bought it at the butcher throughout the year; children grew up without ever discovering what it was like to be truly hungry; fincas increased in value from a 100,000 pesetas to 500,000, to a million, to five million; bicycles gave way to Mobylettes, Mobylettes to Seat 600s, Seat 600s to a bewildering choice of gleaming, luxurious cars; men left the land and worked in the bars, restaurants, hotels, discothèques, the women left their homes during the day and worked in the hotels and the homes of the thousands of foreigners . . .

The Swinnertons discovered a bitter truth: as Canute had known, it was impossible to slow down or stop the tides. He had never bothered to have his investments managed, naïvely assuming that what had been good in the past would be good in the future, and some of his shares had become virtually valueless and others hadn't appreciated as much as was necessary in times of inflation. As his income remained, at best, steady, prices and wages soared. Wine which had been ten pesetas a bottle rose to eighty. The gardeners demanded a hundred pesetas an hour, then a hundred and fifty; soon, it was two hundred . . . There came a time when the Swinnertons were finally forced to face the facts. If things continued in the same vein, before long they'd no longer be able to afford to live in their house. And when they couldn't and had to sell—for a price which would not reflect inflation because no Mallorquin would now live in such isolation and all those foreigners with money lived by the sea—they would be faced with moving into a tiny, noisy, stifling flat or returning to the UK.

At first, Valerie had thought it was the worry about their future which was making her husband look so drawn and had suddenly aged him, but initially she could not discuss the matter because he had tried to shield her from the facts and she did not want him to realize that she was just as aware of them as he. Then, with icy certainty, she had realized there must be something physically wrong with him. He'd tried to evade any medical examination, but in the end had been persuaded to see a specialist in Palma; the specialist diagnosed cancer.

On the morning of the day he'd died, he had looked out of the window and up the terracing and had whispered the wish that he could be buried up there, among all the free beauty instead of the confines of a cemetery. She had told him he was being ridiculous to talk about burials, while silently swearing to honour his wish.

The law on the island concerning burials was strict, as it had to be with the heat in summer, and it did not permit a burial away from an authorized cemetery. But he had died in his own bed and it was not the custom for a doctor to pursue a case if he was not specifically called in by the patient, so that the doctor who had been treating him would never on his own initiative call to find out how he was. In any case, she would have defied a thousand laws in order to carry out her unspoken deathbed promise. So somehow she had managed to carry his emaciated body up to the terrace with the twisted, tortured, centuries-old olive tree which he had nicknamed the Laocöon, and there had buried him.

By then, there was only one gardener—the younger of the two—and he was simple-minded. He'd once asked how the señor was and had then forgotten the subject. And up on that terrace, David Swinnerton's body remained undisturbed, amid the wild beauty he had so loved . . .

'Señora.'

The call cut across her sad, yet comforting thoughts. She looked around and watched the gardener approach with his shambling walk.

He came to a stop. 'Señora.'

She waited patiently. Tomás Mesquida so often had trouble in expressing himself.

'I need . . .' He fiddled with his thick lips. 'I need more money.'

'I'm sorry, but I can't pay you any more.' Her Spanish was fairly fluent, though her accent was poor.

'My mother says I must have more or I stop.'

The foreigners had taught the Mallorquins to be avaricious and now money had become their god. To point out to Mesquida's mother that it would be very difficult for him to find another job and therefore it was surely better to continue to work here for a slightly lesser wage, would be a waste of words; she would never understand that something definite was better than the image of something more. Valerie turned, flinched at the stab of pain from her gouty foot, looked up at the twisted olive tree. If he left, the garden would quickly revert to a wilderness because she could no longer do the work.

Mesquida waited, then, when she remained silent, went over to his rusty Renault 4. He stood by the car for quite a while, as if expecting to be called back, opened the door, settled behind the wheel, drove off.

She turned and, limping slightly, went into the house. There was the sound of the old grandfather clock—one of the pieces they'd brought from Wales—striking the half hour. It reminded her that she was meeting the Attrays for coffee. Since her husband's death, she'd seen quite a bit of the few English residents who lived in, or near, Estruig, rightly judging that for her own mental sake she needed human contacts. In any case, she'd never been the natural recluse that he had.

She went upstairs to the bathroom to find there was no water. Slowly, and most of the time painfully, she returned downstairs and went out to the pump. It was becoming more and more of an effort to work it and normally each weekday Mesquida filled the tank on the roof. If he left her, she'd have to do it all herself . . . An electricity line had come within a kilometre of the house a couple of years before

and the electricity company had asked them if they wanted
to be connected. The estimate had come to two million
pesetas . . .

Twenty-five minutes later she left the house and went
down to the small stone shed in which she garaged the
ancient Seat 850 which was kept going by faith, hope, and
the charity of the garage who so often didn't fully charge
her for the work they'd done.

She drove down the often precipitous road to Estruig,
which was built on and around a small hill that stood a
kilometre away from the mountains. She parked in the main
square, crossed to the café, and looked for the Attrays, but
they were not there. She wasn't surprised. They were very
poor timekeepers. She sat at a table, newly vacated, and
picked up a copy of *El Día* which had been left on it.
She could read Spanish quite well. On the fourth page,
underneath a lurid description of a suicide, complete with
photograph, there was a short article which said that the
man who had died in the car crash near Fogufol had been
identified as Steven Thompson, an Englishman. Her expression became bitter.

CHAPTER 7

Mike Taylor replaced the telephone on its stand, turned,
rested his elbows on the bar. Whoever had said that life on
the island consisted of one long crisis was dead right. Not
very long ago, he'd been wondering how in hell they'd ever
pay for the alterations in the kitchen which the bloody
inspector had demanded be done before they received their
licence to open the restaurant (there was little doubt, but
no proof, that the inspector had been prompted by one or
more of the established restaurant owners), and no sooner
had that problem been solved than he was presented with

a fresh one. His work permit had just been refused. True, his lawyer said that they'd probably win the appeal, but there was bound to be delay. And unless they opened soon, they'd miss the main season which was when any tourist-based business had to make enough profit to last through the rest of the year. He looked through the nearest window at the bay. That view was worth a fortune. Diners with any souls would sit outside, in the shade of the palm trees, staring at so much beauty that they'd never notice whether the meat was tough—what meat in Mallorca wasn't?—and would feel impelled to order another bottle of wine . . .

'Well, is the maître d' satisfied?'

He turned to face Helen as she stood in the doorway of the kitchen. 'If you're interested, I'm thinking of committing suicide.'

'If you come to a decision, do it outside; so much easier to clean up the mess.'

'I'd die much happier if I knew I'd died a bloody nuisance.'

She left the doorway, went behind the bar, put her hands round the back of his neck and brought his head forward so that she could kiss him. 'What total disaster has occurred this time?'

'That call was from Ferrer. They've refused the work permit.'

'No.'

'Bloody yes.'

'Oh well, I suppose we shouldn't have expected it to go through first time. Stop worrying. Pablo will sort it all out.'

'Why are you always revoltingly optimistic?'

'It makes life more fun.'

'I suppose you do realize that if we don't get a work permit . . .'

'Relax. We will. I've complete faith in Pablo.'

'I don't suppose you know how he feels about you?'

'Someone told me that his nickname's Don Juan.'

'If he ever dares make a move in your direction, his nickname will become Doña Juana.'

She chuckled as she unclasped her hands and stepped back. 'I've nearly finished. When did the builders promise faithfully on the pain of excommunication to start work?'

'Yesterday.'

'Then there's just a chance, I suppose, they'll turn up tomorrow . . . As soon as I have finished, let's go for a swim?'

'Slacking?'

'That's right,' she said, happy to see that his black mood was beginning to lift.

He watched her return into the kitchen, lit a cigarette. A year ago he'd been bumming around the world, weighed down by the chip on his shoulder. In the tiny fishing village of Amozgat, in the south-west corner of Turkey, he'd fallen ill with some kind of intestinal infection so severe that he'd become convinced he was dying; a conviction which the villagers had obviously shared and which equally obviously had not caused them any concern beyond the problems that his death might raise vis-à-vis the authorities. On the third day, when death would have been welcome, Helen had appeared in the squalid, stinking room and had nursed him with a devotion which was extraordinary since they were strangers, she was not a trained nurse, and the side effects of his illness were highly unpleasant. Later, he'd learned that her presence in the village had been pure chance. She'd been travelling a hundred miles to the north, had stopped at a café for coffee, and had heard one of the other customers mention the name Amozgat. For some reason, still completely inexplicable, she had been overwhelmed by the certainty that she must visit this place whose name she had only just heard . . . But for that, he might have died and she would in all probability have returned to the man from whom she'd fled two months before . . .

All right, so fate moved in mysterious ways. But why in hell had it moved to turn down his work permit?

She returned to the restaurant. 'Let's go.'

They went out by the kitchen door, walked round the building, past the patio and the palm trees, across the road, and on to the sand. She took off her T-shirt and shorts to reveal a bikini; he was wearing trunks.

He was a much stronger swimmer than she and while she stayed within her depth—which, because the sea bed shelved so gradually was almost two hundred metres out— he continued on, enjoying the coolness of the water which had not yet warmed to tepid summer heat. Off the harbour, a large yacht was hoisting her spinnaker and as he watched the light wind began to balloon the multi-coloured sail. One day, when they were so successful that people came from as far away as Palma for a meal, he'd buy a yacht and name her *Helen*; she'd be the most beautiful craft afloat. He turned and, no longer employing a powerful crawl, swam slowly inshore. He thought how strange it was that now he should care so much for someone else when previously he'd been careful to care for nobody because experience had taught him that to care was to be rejected . . .

He reached her and they returned to shore. They stretched out on towels, rapidly drying in the hot sun. When the restaurant was a success, they'd shut up in the winter and he'd take her to Hongkong, Bali, Tonga . . .

'What are you thinking?' she asked.

'That when we're rich, I'm going to take you to all the glamorous places in the world.'

She reached out for his hand. 'I don't give a damn if it's Clacton-on-Sea, provided you're there.'

She was looking vulnerable, he thought, and he knew a fierce desire to protect her. Her character was a strange mixture of toughness and tenderness; no one could have been tougher than she in that Turkish fishing village, yet sentimentally she was weak.

They were silent for a while, then she said: 'I saw your stepmother when I was in the port earlier on. I wonder what she was doing in this part of the island?'

'Slumming. Did she deign to notice you?'

'She was on the other side of the road and I doubt she even saw me. She was with that friend of hers—what's his name?'

'The Honourable Archibald Wheeldon.'

'He's very handsome.'

'And wet.'

'Her clothes were really lovely; they must have cost a fortune.'

'She's no idea that one can buy a dress for less than five hundred guineas.'

'Mike, why do you two dislike each other so much?'

'I've told you before, it's traditional to dislike one's stepmother.'

'It's more than that. And it's such a pity.'

Such a pity the bitch didn't fall over the edge of her patio and break her neck. He could still remember, with bitter irony, the words his father had used when he'd first talked about his forthcoming second marriage. Beautiful, charming, generous, kind . . . His father had used words with such abandon and skill that people had accused him not merely of having kissed the Blarney Stone, but of having swallowed it whole. His father had got things very wrong with Muriel. She might be beautiful and charming—if she could be bothered—but she wasn't generous or kind . . .

He'd cleared out of her home just one step ahead of being told to clear out. That's when he'd begun his drifting which had ended in the village of Amozgat. It was funny—funny incredible—that not long ago he had managed to talk himself into believing Muriel would help him and Helen to buy the restaurant. It showed to what lengths self-deception could go. After all, in her eyes people who ran restaurants were on the butt end of the social scale. Yet he'd taken

Helen to see her and to ask for the loan—the loan, not the gift—of six million pesetas. She'd treated Helen with disdain and him with sardonic dislike; she'd said that she was very sorry, but she couldn't afford to help, certain that he knew full well she could have given him twice that amount without the slightest problem. Her contemptuous refusal had so infuriated him that he'd cursed the whole idea into oblivion. It had been Helen who had talked him round, stoutly declaring that somehow, somewhere, they'd find the six million . . . And they had!

'I suppose we ought to move,' she said.

'I suppose.'

'I could easily become as indolent as most of the foreigners out here.'

'You're far too intelligent.'

'For those few kind words, thank you. And next time you call me weak-minded for making a nonsense of my figures, I'll remind you of them.' She sat up. 'Come on, back to work.'

'They must have had a tyrant like you overseeing the building of the Pyramids.'

They returned to the restaurant and just before she went into the kitchen, he looked at his watch. 'I might find Carlos if I went along now.'

'Why not? And persuade him that once we're open, we want the vegetables picked much younger than they usually do.'

'I'll try, but you know what we're up against—if you don't grow it as big as it'll go, you're throwing away good money.'

He left and went round to the shed in which they kept the Vespino which he used when there was no need for the Citroën van. The Vespino proved difficult to start and as he pushed down the pedal for the fifth time, to no avail, he decided that the moment the restaurant proved successful, he'd buy a Volvo. He grinned. If he were to honour all his recent pledges, they'd have to start up a whole chain of restaurants . . .

Puerto Llueso lay to the east and it was appropriate that the first building he passed was a block of flats under construction, since for the past two years there had been an ever increasing rate of development. In one respect, this could be welcome. The more people, the more potential customers. But now the extent of building had reached the stage where it threatened to destroy the whole charm of the port, a charm largely based on sleepy smallness. Could not those responsible see that the development contained the seeds of destruction?

Ballester's finca lay between the port and Llueso, three-quarters of a kilometre back from the main road. Two years previously, he'd been left a little money and he'd used this to have a well drilled. He'd been very lucky. They'd struck flowing water that was sweet and not tainted by sea-water, as so much was now that more and more fresh water was extracted from existing sources to service the tourist industry and the natural water table was dropping. He was young, which was unusual since few young men now went into farming or horticulture because the work was so much harder and less well remunerated than were jobs in the tourist industry; even more unusually, he was ready and eager to learn new methods.

He was working a rotovator when Taylor arrived. He stopped this, crossed the brick-hard land, shook hands with traditional courtesy, talked about the weather. It was almost ten minutes before Taylor was able to introduce the subject of the vegetables. Ballester listened, thought, finally said that he thought it might be possible; then he added that the vegetables would, of course, have to cost a bit more . . .

Taylor returned to the port. He stopped at a newsagent to buy an English paper, but all these had been sold and he had to be content with the *Daily Bulletin*. He continued on to one of the front cafés where prices were merely high and not exorbitant and sat at one of the outside tables. He stared across the road at the yachts in the harbour and he thought about his earlier promise to himself . . .

A waiter asked him what he wanted. He replied in good Spanish—he was a natural linguist—that he'd like a café cortado. After the waiter had left, he began to read the paper. On the second page, it stated that the Englishman who'd been killed in the car crash near Fogufol had been identified as Steven Thompson. His expression abruptly changed.

CHAPTER 8

The Telex message arrived at ten-thirty on Monday morning. Reference the request for identification of the next-of-kin of Steven Arnold Thompson, passport number C 229570 A. This passport was one of twenty-five which had been stolen before issue some four years previously. An examination of records showed no Steven Arnold Thompson. It was, therefore, impossible to advise on next-of-kin.

London added that they would be grateful if they were informed should any details come to light as to how the deceased had come into possession of this stolen passport and they would in due course welcome the opportunity to examine it.

'That,' said Alvarez to a passing fly, 'is not going to make Salas's day.'

'I suppose I should have expected it,' said Salas over the telephone.

'Señor . . .'

'It doesn't matter how simple a case is beforehand, the

moment you have anything to do with it, the complications start.'

'Señor, I really cannot be blamed . . .'

'How much do we know about the dead man?'

'Very little, I'm afraid.'

'Why?'

'Because the only person apart from the man who hired him the car and the porter at the hotel—and their evidence is virtually useless—who I've been able to find who knew him is Señor Higham. He's in hospital because he was in the crash . . .'

'To save time, please assume I have taken the trouble to acquaint myself with the basic facts of the case.'

'Yes, señor. Unfortunately, there's very little that Señor Higham could tell me. Señor Thompson—according to the three of them—flew in from somewhere where it was noticeably colder than here, he owned a boat, he was gregarious but yet a little secretive at the same time, and he suffered from migraine.'

'Are you suggesting that these details are of the greatest importance?'

'No, señor; I said they weren't. But I wanted to illustrate how little I've been able to find out.'

'Have no fear on that score.'

'But he said nothing personal . . .'

'Has it not occurred to you that he must have said more to the hitch-hiker than that.'

'I know it sounds reasonable . . .'

'Which is, no doubt, why you are so reluctant to accept the conclusion. Question him again and this time do so thoroughly.'

'You don't think . . .'

'Will you kindly obey my orders without arguing.'

'Yes, señor. I'll drive in to Palma tomorrow morning and . . .'

'You will drive in this morning.'

'But I have a great deal of work in hand.'

'I want this matter cleared up and cleared up quickly.' The line went dead.

Alvarez replaced the receiver. He'd planned a quiet day. But now he had to rush into Palma and question Higham again, when it was perfectly clear to anyone but a mule-headed superior chief that it would be a complete waste of time. He sighed.

The door banged open and a guard walked in, dropped a large brown envelope on to the desk, held out a sheet of paper. 'Sign this.'

'What is it?'

'It's come from Palma on the bus and they want a receipt. That's all I know.'

Alvarez signed and the guard left. He stared doubtfully at the envelope for several seconds—it was his experience that communications direct from Palma were seldom of a pleasant nature—finally opened it. Inside was a British passport and a wallet. He opened the passport. Jack Higham, accounts clerk, born in London on 21 October, 1941, residence England; height, 1.80 cms; signature a bit of a scrawl; photograph the usual stark, unflattering reproduction which left Higham's face almost expressionless.

He checked the wallet. No money, of course. No credit cards. A couple of stamps, a receipt from a hostal, a list of numbers with some crossed off, and a photograph of a woman who was laughing. The wife who had run off with another man because she couldn't take the bad times as well as the good? He replaced the photograph. If she were the wife, then the fact that Higham had kept it showed that his casual acceptance of all that had happened was a mask, concealing his true emotions. Poor sod, thought Alvarez, knowing what it was like to suffer.

He returned both wallet and passport to the brown envelope.

*

Higham was sitting in the armchair near the window, to the side of the settee. His colour was much better and the bruising on his chin had almost disappeared. Alvarez handed him the copy of the *Daily Mail* which he had just bought.

'That's really decent of you.'

He sat on the edge of the bed, produced the brown envelope and emptied out the wallet and passport. 'These were dropped into a litter-bin, here, in Palma.'

'Good God!'

'Im afraid all the money's gone. What happens is, the thief takes everything he wants, then drops the rest. That way, he gets rid of any incriminating evidence at virtually no risk to himself.' By leaning forward, Alvarez was able to pass them across. Higham flicked through the passport, then checked each compartment of the wallet.

'Have you spoken to the consul and asked him about the money?'

'Yes, I did; that is I phoned and spoke to someone who knew what I was talking about. She'll contact the bank who issued the travellers' cheques and tell them they've been stolen. One problem was, I couldn't say which ones I'd cashed.' He tapped the wallet. 'But I've a note of them here and I'll ring her again and give the numbers.'

'I hope the refund will come through quickly.'

'They always promise it will . . . You know, I've done a lot of thinking since I've been in here and I'm seeing things straighter. At my age, drifting around Europe won't change anything or get me anywhere; I've got too old for the dream. I need to return home and find another job; and perhaps meet someone . . .' He tailed off into silence and stared out through the window.

'I am very sorry that your visit to the island has been so unfortunate.'

'It has, hasn't it? But even so, I'm going to come back as soon as I can. It's so beautiful.'

'Then next time, I hope that nothing happens to spoil your pleasure.'

'I'll drink to that!' He smiled. 'One thing, I'll not try thumbing a lift.'

There was a short silence which Alvarez broke. 'Señor, I am sorry, but I have to ask you more questions. You see, because we did not know who Señor Thompson's next-of-kin was, we sent the number of his passport back to England and asked them to give us what information they could. They have reported that his passport was one which had been stolen, along with others, before it was issued.'

'Well, I'll be damned!'

'So now we are back to knowing almost nothing about him, but we need to trace his next-of-kin.'

'I don't see how I can help there.'

'Perhaps he said something which at the time seemed of no importance, and so you didn't bother to mention it when I spoke to you before, but which might help me now. For instance, where had he been driving from that morning?'

'I don't know.'

'And I think you told me, he didn't say where he was going?'

'He didn't, no.'

'Nor did he give you any hint of why he was on the island?'

'I'm not so certain about that. You see, there's something tickling my mind . . .' There was a longish silence before Higham continued: 'He mentioned something about having been driving around the island, seeing people. I asked him if he was on business. He laughed.'

'Did you understand why he should laugh at that question?'

'No. Your guess is as good as mine.'

'So either for some reason the question held an amusing connotation or it was the answer that did—the answer he didn't make.'

'It must have been something like that.'

'Did he ever mention the name of anyone on the island?'

'No.'

'Or any place?'

'No.'

'But he did tell you he'd visited the island before?'

'That's right.'

'Did he make any reference to the previous visits?'

'No.'

'Or talk about his home life?'

'Not a word.'

'So although he was a talkative man, he hardly told you anything about himself?'

'That sums it up.'

'D'you think he was being deliberately secretive?'

'I wouldn't like to say one way or the other.'

'You didn't gain any kind of an impression?'

'Look, you're asking me a whole load of questions I just can't answer.'

'No, of course not. But as I mentioned earlier, it's just that sometimes one can look back and realize one gained an impression, even though at the time one wasn't aware that one had.'

'Not this time.'

'So then it seems that maybe he'll remain a man with no background. All we shall ever know about him is that he flew in from somewhere, he'd been here before, perhaps was here on business, enjoyed sailing, suffered from migraine, and it was an attack of this which indirectly killed him.'

'In fact, not even that's certain.'

'How d'you mean?'

'Because . . . Well, I'm damned!' Higham's voice expressed his astonishment. 'It's funny how the memory works, isn't it? I've only this moment remembered that after he'd decided to take another pill—because the earlier one wasn't doing any good—and we'd driven off and he started feeling ill, he said no migraine had ever been like that before; his mouth and throat were burning as if he'd chewed half a dozen of the vicious little peppers which grow on the island and on top of that he didn't have any of the usual symptoms. He wondered if some of the food at the restaurant had been bad. But he'd only had steak and ice-cream . . . And then, like I said before, he was as sick as a dog, but would carry on driving. It's funny how life goes, isn't it? If he'd been more ill, he couldn't have gone on driving; if less ill, he'd have been able to keep control.'

Alvarez's mind flicked back over the years. If Juana-María had walked fractionally quicker or slower, the drunken Frenchman would not have pinned her to the wall with his car . . . He stood.

'You surely don't have to go yet awhile?'

'I am afraid so. It is still lonely for you?'

'And frustrating! There's a new night nurse who could be fun, but she doesn't understand a word of English.'

'I have heard that in such circumstances it is possible to communicate the essentials with signs.'

'I tried, but we don't seem to speak the same sign language.'

Alvarez smiled. 'How much longer will you have to stay here?'

'I'm feeling fit enough to leave now, but the quack says he still can't understand why I suffered a loss of memory at the beginning so he wants to make absolutely certain I didn't suffer any brain damage. I told him, only softening of the brain. He didn't see the joke and it took a hell of a long time trying to explain it . . . I guess the Spanish and English senses of humour aren't very similar.'

'That is very true . . . Señor, should you remember anything more, however unimportant it seems to you, will you get in touch with me?'

'Sure. But how do I get hold of you?'

'I will give you my home and office telephone numbers.

If you say my name, whoever answers will know to get hold
of me if I'm around.' He wrote out the numbers, handed
the piece of paper over, said goodbye and left.

The telephone rang at six-thirty that evening, just as Alvarez
was wondering whether it really was too early to leave the
office and return home.

'It's Cantallops here, Inspector.'

'Who?'

'The undertaker from Fogufol. You must remember—I
rang you the other day.'

'Oh yes, of course.'

'I want to know if it's all right now to go ahead with the
funeral?'

'There's no reason why not. What name are you going to
use?'

'Thompson, of course. What are you on about?'

'He was travelling on a stolen passport so the odds probably are that that's not his real name. But then I don't
suppose St Peter will keep the gates shut just because he's
buried under the wrong name.'

'That's ridiculous.'

'I don't see why. Surely by then the name's quite unimportant?'

'It's ridiculous to say his name wasn't Thompson.'

'Why is it?'

'His son would have told me if it wasn't.'

'His son? Here, you'd better tell me what's been going
on.'

'Nothing's been going on. Why do you people always
suspect everybody and everything?'

'Because that's what we're paid for . . . But just for the
moment, I'm not suspecting you of anything specific. All I
want to know is, how come you've heard from the son?'

'There was this phone call. The son had just learned of
the tragic death of his father and he wanted to know what

arrangements there were for the funeral. I told him there weren't any. He said his father was to be decently and honourably buried.'

'When did you receive this call?'

'Saturday.'

'Why didn't you get on to me right away?'

'The money hadn't arrived then.'

'What are you talking about now?'

'Until I had the money, I couldn't go ahead and arrange the funeral, could I?'

'Depends what kind of a man you are . . . How much?'

There was a slight pause. 'Two hundred and fifty thousand pesetas.'

'Has the son ordered a gold coffin?'

'He asked me to prepare an honourable funeral.'

'How are you getting in touch with him to let him know the time of the honourable funeral?'

'I'm not. He said it was quite impossible for him to come over from England because of family problems . . . May I go ahead and arrange everything?'

'Yes. And then get back on to me with all the details.'

Alvarez replaced the receiver. He stared through the open window. Thompson had been travelling on a stolen passport and so it was reasonable to assume that Thompson was not his real name. The report of his death had been in the local papers, but was unlikely to have appeared in the British national papers. Then how had the son learned that he had died in the car accident?

CHAPTER 9

The present cemetery at Fogufol was three-quarters of a kilometre outside the village, reached by a narrow, twisting lane. From it, there was a view across the central plain of the island and, especially after rain, the sea to the south-east was clearly visible. The high surrounding stone walls had been erected in the eighteenth century, the chapel and room of remembrance in the late nineteenth. Originally, the graves had been marked merely by single headstones, but then the custom had arisen of spending on death more than had ever been spent on life and headstones had become large and elaborate, while those families with property had erected mausoleums. The land was stone, making excavation both difficult and costly, and therefore there were no single graves; always, there was a shaft and excavated out on either side of this were cubicles into which coffins could be fitted.

The cemetery was, of course, for Catholics and the first non-Catholic to die within the parish—a German botanist —had presented the priest and the council with a problem. The law said that the dead had to be buried within consecrated ground, the Church said that only a Catholic could be buried within the cemetery. In the end it was decided that just before he died, and even though he'd been alone when he'd fallen fifteen metres on to his head, the German had expressed the wish to become a Roman Catholic and therefore it was in order to bury him within the cemetery. Since then, the number of foreigners, many of them non-Catholics, had risen very considerably and it had become clear that since deaths must be expected, an elegant solution for one must become an inelegant, not to say absurd, solution for many. Eventually, it was decided to provide an area of consecrated ground outside the actual cemetery where all non-Catholics could be buried. A deep shaft, which accommodated six cubicles on either side, was blasted out of the rock and above this was built a sandstone edifice which resembled an old-fashioned steamer trunk; on the sides of this were plaques on which, for a suitable fee, the names of the deceased could be inscribed. When the last cubicle was filled, the first one was emptied and the bones were taken out and stored with the bones of those locals who had died well back in the past; in death there was no equality, in disintegration there was.

Religion raised one further question. Where was the burial ceremony to be held? The solution of the Fogufol priest, a traditionalist who viewed the spirit of œcumenicism in a less than happy light, was to ask that it be held under the archway of the entrance; after all, Moses had been allowed to view the Promised Land.

Alvarez parked next to the Citroën 2CV van, as battered as his 600, in front of a narrow flowerbed which ran the length of the cemetery wall. He walked slowly to the arched entrance to the cemetery. There were very few people present. The Anglican churchman was pacing backwards and forwards, a puzzled look on his ancient, lined, and toothy face; each time he reached the outer side of the archway, he came to a stop and stared up the path, seeking a press of people which never materialized. The undertaker and two assistants waited lethargically on one side, three men employed by the local council even more lethargically on the other. Taylor, his rugged face set in sullen lines, dressed in open shirt and cotton trousers, stood by the doorway into the chapel.

Cicadas shrilled, a hoopoe hooped, sheep bells clanged, and dogs barked. The clergyman cleared his throat as he looked at his watch. 'Perhaps we should begin the service.' He picked up a pile of printed sheets and handed these around; the council employees and the undertakers refused them. The clergyman announced the first hymn, la-di-dahed the tune, and then led the singing; it turned out to be a solo.

Alvarez studied the young man. He was casually dressed, as if he could not be bothered to offer the deceased any respect, yet his expression was unmistakably sad and, perhaps, resentful, in the sense that the living sometimes resented the fact that the dead had left them . . . The son had told Cantallops over the phone that he could not come to the funeral and this man's face was bronzed, whereas almost all newly arrived visitors from Britain were white, yet if the son did live in England there was still no obvious answer to the question, how had he learned of his father's death?

The clergyman announced that a last prayer would be said at the graveside and left. Taylor followed him. Alvarez returned to his car, opened both doors and sat, beads of sweat sliding down his cheeks and back to make him feel still more sticky and uncomfortable.

After a while, Taylor walked out of the archway and across to the Citroën van. As he opened the driving door, Alvarez called out. Taylor looked at him for a moment, climbed in behind the wheel, slammed the door shut. Alvarez crossed to the van as the starter engine engaged, but the engine refused to fire. 'One moment, please, señor.'

'What d'you want?'

'First, to know your name.'

'How the hell's that any of your business?'

'Cuerpo General de Policía.'

'So?'

'So I would like to know your name, please.'

'Where's your identity card?'

'My what?'

'Your card, proving you are a detective.'

Alvarez spoke with astonishment. 'Would I be here, on a day this hot, attending the funeral of a man I never knew, if I were not?'

'How do I know what anyone on this crazy island will do?'

'Your papers, please.'

'Look, I'm here for a funeral. That's all.'

'Of course. I would still like to see them.'

Taylor reached across to the locker and brought out of this a heavy-duty plastic envelope which, sullenly, he passed across.

Alvarez briefly checked the insurance papers, yearly

licence, and photostat copy of a Spanish driving licence. 'Your name is Michael Taylor and your address is Calle Llube, number fifteen, Puerto Llueso?'

'That's what written down.'

'Do you know that you should have with you your original licence and not a photostat copy?'

Taylor did not answer.

'Do you have a residencia?'

'Yes. And to save the question, it's at home.'

'You should carry that with you as well.'

'Look, if I did everything the law demands, I'd be schizo-phrenic.'

'Why have you come here this morning?'

'I'd have thought that was obvious, even to you.'

'Señor, I can quietly ask questions here, or I can demand that you come to the nearest guardia post where I'll ask them rather more loudly.'

Belatedly, Taylor realized that his sullenly provocative attitude was hardly a sensible one. 'I came to the funeral.'

'You knew Señor Thompson?'

'Yes.'

'Did you know him well?'

'No.'

'Yet you have come all the way from Puerto Llueso to attend his funeral?'

'I reckoned there ought to be someone here to see him buried.'

'Then you knew there would not be anyone else—how?'

Taylor shrugged his shoulders.

'Was it because you were aware that he was being buried under a false name?'

'I met him a couple of times and that's it. I've no idea what his private life was about.'

'When did you last speak to him?'

'I don't really remember.'

'How did you know the funeral was to be today?'

'Someone said it was.'

'Who?'

'I don't remember whom.'

Alvarez stared at the ground for several seconds, then looked up as he stepped back. 'Thank you for your help, señor.'

Taylor was clearly surprised, and relieved, at this sudden termination of the questioning. He engaged the starter again and this time the engine fired. He drove off, the engine emitting the typical high-pitched scream.

Alvarez returned to the 600. He sat, switched on the fan. Sweet Mary, but it was hot!

Dolores poured out a second cup of coffee for Alvarez, then went over to the doorway and shouted to Juan and Isabel that if they didn't get a move on, they'd be late for school. Safe from immediate chastisement, Juan replied that he didn't care.

'I don't know what's happening,' she grumbled, as she returned to the table. 'When I was young, I wouldn't have dreamt of speaking to my mother like that.'

'When we were young, things were very different.'

She recalled a life so hard that in comparison with the present it seemed as if her memory must be playing her false. Had there really been times when her parents simply could not properly feed the large family; had there been so much fear on the streets that only a fool ever said what was in his mind?

He spoke slowly. 'If only some of the things which were worthwhile had not been destroyed along with so much that was bad.' It might be utterly futile, but nothing could prevent his regretting the present lack of inner discipline and inner pride which together had kept a poor man's head held as high as a rich man's.

She was unconcerned with these aspects of past and present; not for her the problems which lay outside the family. 'No matter, I've no time to stand about and chatter, like a cluck hen. And you ought to have left for work half an hour ago.'

'Would you have me kill myself from overwork?'

She laughed scornfully, picked up a duster, left and went through to the dining-room. He drank the coffee and thought about Taylor. It was easy to mistake most emotions, but surely sorrow was difficult to misread. Taylor had been sorrowing. Then the relationship between himself and the dead man had surely been son and father and it had been he who had paid for the funeral . . .

Twenty-five minutes later, he telephoned Cantallops from the office.

'Where did the money come from?' said Cantallops.

'Where the hell d'you think?'

'Was it paid in cash, by cheque, or by bank draft?'

'I can't remember.'

'Then go and look.'

Cantallops swore, put the phone down. When he next spoke, he said: 'It was transferred direct into my account.'

'From which bank?'

'I don't know. You've more damn questions than a dog's got fleas.'

'Which, I can assure you, are no less irritating. Will you give me your authorization to find out from your bank where the money came from?'

'If I have to.'

CHAPTER 10

Calle Llube had, twenty years before, been the last road in Puerto Llueso; now there stretched beyond it one large urbanización, completed, and a second one under construction. It was a road of one-floor buildings, all with simple, bleak exteriors in which the only hint of beauty was in the window-boxes filled with flowers. However, behind their road fronts there was considerably more space and comfort than a casual observer would have thought; some had enclosed patios in which grew flowers and, occasionally, orange trees.

Alvarez stepped through the bead curtain of No. 15 and called out. A short, fat woman with an ugly but humorous face came into the room. He asked to speak to Taylor.

'He'll be at the restaurant.'

'But he does live here?'

'Rents the two rooms at the back.' She indicated with a quick wave of her pudgy hand the far side of the patio. 'Lives there with his woman.' She spoke with open disapproval. Had he been a Spaniard, let alone a Mallorquin, she would never have let him stay in her house with a woman who was not his wife.

'Where's the restaurant?'

'D'you know Las Cinco Palmeras?'

'Along the bay road?'

'That's it. Bought it and spent a fortune on it, by all accounts, but it's still not open.'

'Has he been with you for long?'

'Since last summer. Look, is something the matter?'

'It's only a question of papers.'

She was relieved—everyone had trouble with papers— since she liked the two of them, even though they weren't married.

He left, drove down to the front and then round the bay to the restaurant. He parked by the side of the patio and climbed out. Behind the buildings were marshland and farmland, some of it incredibly under the Philistine threat of development, which stretched to the encircling mountains; in front was the bay. The perfect site.

A few chairs and tables were stacked to one side of the nearest palm tree; the main door of the restaurant was shut and there was a notice in English and Spanish which stated that the restaurant would be opening at the end of the month. He walked round to the back. The battered Citroën van that he'd seen at the cemetery was parked near a shed. A woman was hanging up chequered tablecloths on a long line and when she saw him she dropped a tablecloth into the bucket and came across. 'Are you from the builders?' she asked in inaccurate, but understandable, Spanish.

'No, I'm not.'

'Blast!' Exasperation forced her into speaking English. 'I suppose that was much too much to ask for since it's only this morning they promised once again to come immediately.'

He said in English: 'We have a saying. A man waits for death and the builders and only death knows which will arrive first.'

'Oh, you understand! Then it's a good job I kept to ladylike language . . . Your saying suggests it's not only the foreigners who suffer.'

'That's right.'

'I know it shouldn't, but that cheers me up a bit . . . If you're not the builder, who are you and how can I help?'

He told her.

She said curiously: 'Mike should be back any moment. He just nipped into the port to buy some paint . . . Is something wrong?'

'I need to ask him a few questions.'

She was about to say something more when they heard the puttering of an approaching Vespino. 'That must be him now.'

Taylor entered the yard and braked the Vespino to a halt, cut the engine, drew the bike back up on its stand, picked out of the wire basket a four-litre tin of paint. It wasn't until he was a third of the way across that he recognized Alvarez; when he did, he came to a stop. Noting his expression, Helen's curiosity and perplexity changed to sharp concern.

'Good morning, señor.'

'What d'you want?' Taylor asked belligerently. 'To see my driving licence because the law says a photostat copy isn't good enough even though I couldn't have one if I didn't have the original?'

'To ask you some questions concerning two hundred and fifty thousand pesetas.'

He hunched his shoulders, as he might have done if expecting to have to ward off a blow.

'Mike . . .' began Helen.

'Look, love, suppose you take the van and find the builders and use all your charm to jerk them into some action?'

'But surely you phoned them only an hour ago . . .'

'Just go, eh?'

'No, I won't.' She walked forward until she could grip his free hand in hers. She had no idea what was wrong, but whatever was the trouble, she was going to share it.

'Perhaps it would be more pleasant if we sat down?' suggested Alvarez.

Taylor looked as if he were obstinately going to refuse to move, then suddenly changed his mind. After releasing his hand, he led the way into the restaurant which was reasonably cool, thanks to the open windows and the slight sea breeze. The tables and chairs had been stacked to one side, leaving three walls clear for painting, and after putting the can down, using more force than was necessary because violent action was one way in which he could release a little of his bitter anger, he moved out one table and three chairs. He sat, deliberately not waiting for them.

Helen, in an attempt to neutralize his all-too-evident antagonism, said to Alvarez: 'Would you like a drink?'

'Thank you, I would very much. Do you have a coñac?'

She went through to the kitchen, to return with a tray on which were three glasses, one with a drink in it, a bottle of 103, and a soda siphon. She put the tray on the table, turned to Alvarez. 'I'm sorry, but we haven't any ice at the moment —the wiring of the kitchen is one of the things we're waiting to have done so neither of the refrigerators is working. It makes me wonder what on earth people did with food in the heat in the old days.'

'There was an ice factory in Llueso and each morning two mule carts brought ice down to the port for the ice-boxes.'

'You've lived here a long time?'

'Long enough to remember the ice-carts, señora, but I wasn't born at this end of the island.'

'When you first came to the port, it must have been quite small?'

'There were the few big houses on the front which belonged to the rich in Palma, one hotel, two or three shops, and many fishermen's cottages.'

'But no memento shops, or tourist bars, or discos . . . It must have been so lovely.'

'Lovely for the rich,' said Taylor. 'While the poor could always feast on the scenery.'

'Mike,' she said, worried.

'What you suggest is true, señor,' said Alvarez pacifically. 'There was much for the few, little for the many; now that has changed, but so has the life. Who can say which is the better?'

'The poor sods who didn't have anything then, but do now.'

'I suppose you are right. And yet . . .'

'Spiritually, so much has been lost?' she suggested.

'Crap!' Taylor said crudely.

'Mike, how can you be so certain that it's always better if the many benefit at the expense not only of the few, but also of the quality of life?'

'Because I've no time for an élitist society unless I'm one of the élite.' He finally poured out two brandies. 'Soda?' he asked Alvarez curtly.

'No, thank you.'

He added soda to his own drink. 'All right, we've sorted

out the problems of the world; now let's sort out yours. What's bugging you if it's not my bloody driving licence?'

'Did you pay two hundred and fifty thousand pesetas to Señor Cantallops for the funeral of Señor Thompson?'

Helen exclaimed: 'So that's why . . .' Abruptly, she stopped.

'No,' said Taylor loudly, 'I didn't.'

'Perhaps I should explain that I have spoken with the manager of the Banco de Bilbao in Foguful and with the manager of the Caja de Ahorros y Monte Piedad de Las Baleares here, in the port.'

'Then why in the hell ask?'

'Why did you pay for the funeral?'

'Is there any law to say I can't?'

'Of course not.'

'Then it's my business.'

'Señor Thompson was travelling on a false passport when he died. Now, I have to find out his true identity. Was he your father?'

Taylor drained his glass, poured himself another, and larger brandy, added soda, drank.

Alvarez produced a pack of cigarettes and offered it; Helen shook her head, Taylor ignored him. He lit a cigarette and waited with the timeless patience that marked his peasant background.

After a while, Taylor said: 'All right, he was my father. Steven Arthur Taylor. One of the Taylors of Chelton Cross, not that you'd get any of the present bunch willingly to acknowledge the fact.'

'Will you tell me about him?'

'Why not? It's amusing in a banana-skin kind of way and it can't hurt him any more.'

His family had been county, large landowners for generations; conscious of their position, yet equally conscious of the obligations this raised. It had become smart to sneer both at the squire and the subservient tenant, but when the system had been in the hands of honourable people it had worked well for both sides; better to touch a forelock than to starve in a town stew. (Taylor's tone expressed the dichotomy of emotions he felt; he admired the squires for what they'd done, held them in contempt for what they'd been.) But time had, as always, demanded change. When Steven Taylor was born, the land remained but the respect had to be earned and did not come as a by-product of the acres.

Steven Taylor had been a cuckoo in the respectable nest. People agreed that it was a mercy of providence that he had not been born the elder son since then he would have inherited the estate and to earn the respect of the staff and tenants it would have been necessary to conform, because they, being countrymen, were great traditionalists, yet from the beginning he had refused to conform. He was born five hours after an eminent gynæcologist had given it as a firm opinion that he wouldn't be for at least forty-eight hours. At his first prep school, the honours system had been in force; pupils were put on their honour not to cheat in their work and were not prevented from doing so by supervision, because this taught them to be true to themselves. When caught cheating, he had tried to explain to the headmaster that under such a system, anyone of intelligence was impelled to cheat because only a foои could ignore the advantages to be gained by so doing. The headmaster had been looking for repentance, not intelligence, and he had been so outraged that he had expelled Steven Taylor even though names from four previous generations of the family were on the Eton Scholarships board. His second prep school, chosen on the grounds that since it was only twenty years old its philosophy would be far more attuned to the sons of the middle class than those of the aristocracy and county, held that every pupil would commit every crime in the book unless prevented from doing so by either force or fear. The three years he'd spent there had taught him that survival called for an ability to think quickly, a gift for lying, and luck.

He went on to Eton, once more back in the mainstream of family tradition. At sixteen and a half, he was found in bed with one of the whores who worked from a house in Gleethorpe Road. The headmaster might, in view of his family history, have found some way of avoiding expelling him had he not, in answer to the question why had he done so degrading and socially dangerous a thing, replied that if degradation was a nineteen-year-old blonde, it was a diffi-cult thing to resist, and honest fornication was surely far less physically dangerous than illegal homosexuality.

Australia no longer quietly received drop-outs from the wealthier families, so it became necessary for the family to decide what to do with him. In view of his known weaknesses —an eagerness to gamble, a disregard for convention, a tendency to lawlessness, the ability to concentrate on the ends and not the means, and an absence of any sense of shame—it was decided to use family influence to get him into a commodity broking firm.

The firm into which he was introduced had one rule that was absolute; no member might trade on his own behalf. At the age of twenty, he used some highly confidential information concerning frost damage in the Brazilian coffee plantations to set up a futures position which netted him half a million pounds. Unfortunately, he paid so much attention to his own affairs that he neglected the firm's and he lost them just under a million in sugar. The senior partner's final words on his departure were that, dishonest and incompetent, he was clearly far better suited to the stock market.

He spent the half million in just under seven years. He sampled everything life had to offer and frequently went back for more. His motto might have been: How could one possibly appreciate what was good without sampling what was evil?

When the last of the money was gone, he was faced with the problem of living. Lacking any sense of shame, he didn't hesitate to approach his elder brother and suggest he join the family trust which ran the land and the growing number of business interests. His brother, a sobersides, a roundhead, a pillar of the establishment, made it quite clear that in his view the father of the prodigal son had been guilty of a grave misjudgement.

Lacking any obvious means of gaining immediate and profitable employment, Steven Taylor accepted that he was left with only one course of action open to him, a course pioneered by the members of the aristocracy. To marry the daughter of a rich man. Even straits more desperate than those he now found himself in would not have persuaded him to marry the majority of such daughters, but Prudence was not only eligible, she was not noticeably spotty. Naturally, he was faced by considerable opposition from other indigent younger sons, but he had one asset none of them possessed, a golden tongue. Three weeks after coming to the decision, when her father was in Florida buying or selling some sort of property, he proposed and was accepted.

When her father returned home and heard about the marriage, he commented angrily on the insolent neck of penniless adventurers who were stupid enough to think he was a soft touch. Nothing more clearly illustrated Steven Taylor's subtlety of tongue (or perhaps it was the naïvety of property tycoons) than the fact that at the end of a two-hour interview, her father had agreed not only to the wedding, but also to continuing and even increasing Prudence's already very generous allowance.

The marriage had not lasted long. She was, even by the standards of her contemporaries, shallow-minded and to his chagrin he'd discovered that not even all her money compensated for her overriding ambition, to appear regularly in the more mindless upmarket social magazines. They parted soon after their son was born and she remarried, this

time to a man of substance—notable head of house at
Harrow, a first in Greats, one of the few Lloyds underwriters
who had never perfected a scheme to fleece his names, on
the invitation lists of all the best hostesses in London.
Strangely, the marriage soon bored her and after a while
she realized that this was because it was so bland and she
had been taught the taste of spice. In angry rebellion, she'd
emptied a bowl of rice crispies over her husband's head. He
never did understand why. Not long afterwards, she'd been
driving back to her flat in London when a drunken youth,
in a stolen Jaguar, had crashed head-on into her car and
killed her.

Steven Taylor had read about her death in a newspaper
and the article reminded him that he had a son.

Mike went to live with his father. Life changed abruptly
and then went on changing, with often heartbreaking
rapidity. One day they'd be rich, the next they'd be poor;
a large house in January, a terrace two up and two down in
July; a new Rover in February, a clapped-out Mini in
August. But far more bewildering than these swings were
those occasioned by his moves from one school to another,
from the private sector to the state one and then back again.
Each time he managed to make friends, it was only to be
wrenched away from them; each time he changed sectors,
he was jeered at by his peers and, until he learned to fight
ferociously, bullied because he came from an alien world.
School taught him that only the strong survive . . .

Then, without any warning, his father had married again.
He'd seen this as a betrayal, even though he was now
more than old enough to have realized that his father was
searching for security. Muriel was the attractive and very
wealthy widow of a much older husband who had originally
employed her as his private secretary and had then discovered that, unlike the previous ones, her price was not to
be computed solely in pounds.

For a time, life had stabilized. A large house near the

small village of Middle Cross, a few miles from Dover, a Philippine couple to run it, a Daimler and a Rover, holidays in exotic places which had not yet been overtaken by *hoi polloi* . . . Sometimes he wondered if his father and he would have settled down if Muriel had not been such a ridiculous snob who had deliberately set out to use her money to humiliate his father because his background was all that hers was not? But such a question was profitless. She was as she was and his father was as he was and life became too painful for him to stay any longer at Keene House . . .

'Did you often see or hear from your father after you left home?' Alvarez asked.

'Never.'

'But you must have had some contact with him?'

'I've just said, never.'

'I find that difficult to understand.'

'Lucky you! No bloody mixed-up feelings towards your own father? You can't see what it was like for me. He was my father, but it was he who was responsible for me having had to keep changing schools. Ever had a crowd of kids jeering at you simply because you speak with a different accent from them; and feeling so alone you wanted to die then and there? It was he who married Muriel and gave her the chance to humiliate him because she'd got the money and he hadn't.'

'You're saying that you hated him?'

'It's not so simple that one word can describe it. I loved him even as I was humiliated because he allowed himself to be humiliated by Muriel. I looked up to him, but . . .'

'But what?'

'Leave him alone,' said Helen fiercely. 'Can't you see how it hurts to talk about it?'

Alvarez changed the line of his questioning. 'But you did meet your father on this island?'

'Yes.'

'How often?'

'Twice.'

'Roughly when was this?'

Taylor shrugged his shoulders. 'Three or four months ago, then a month.'

'Didn't you see him at the beginning of last week?'

'I didn't even know he was back on the island.'

'How did he first learn you were living here?'

'Through Muriel; she lives on the island now.'

'You'd kept in touch with her?'

'When Helen and I decided to try to buy this restaurant, I was fool enough to go to her to borrow the money.'

'She refused?'

'Naturally.'

'Why d'you say that?'

'Imagine the blot on her social escutcheon if her stepson were to run a tourist restaurant.'

'She's so wrong,' said Helen.

'Of course she's bloody wrong,' he said bitterly. 'But she won't even consider heaven until she's convinced that only the right people are admitted.'

'Did you know that your father was travelling on a false passport?' Alvarez asked.

'I knew he'd changed his name.'

'Did this surprise you?'

'Nothing he did surprised me.'

'Why did he change his name?'

'I've no idea.'

'You didn't ask him?'

'No.'

'You weren't at all curious?'

'I've learned to mind my own business and leave other people to mind theirs.'

'He never gave even a hint of what the reason was?'

'No.'

Alvarez was certain that Taylor was lying, but equally certain that for the moment nothing would persuade him to tell the truth. 'Thank you for all your help, señor. And I am very sorry if it has been painful for you, but I promise you that I had to ask the questions.'

Taylor made no reply, nor did he look up when Alvarez stood. But Helen followed Alvarez out into the yard and his car. 'He didn't mean to be rude,' she said earnestly, worried that he had taken offence at the aggressive way in which Taylor had spoken. 'It's just that he's had such a difficult life and he normally hates talking about it. Today's the first time I've heard some of the things he's just told you.'

'I understand.'

She studied him. 'Yes, you really do. Thank you.'

As he opened the car door and climbed in behind the wheel, he thought how strange it was that she should think it necessary to thank him for understanding that no man could ever separate himself from his past.

Alvarez spoke to Superior Chief Salas over the telephone. 'His real name was Steven Arthur Taylor. He'd been married twice and was clearly a bit of a rogue, but by default rather than intention.'

'What is that supposed to mean?'

'Well, that . . . What I'm trying to say is that I'm certain he didn't have vicious motives, he just didn't find the same dividing line between right and wrong that you and I do.'

'The practical difference escapes me. Send the information to London.'

'I've already done so.'

'You have?' Salas sounded surprised. 'Then the matter can be closed and you can return all your energies to your normal work.' He cut the connection.

Alvarez settled back in his chair and stared resentfully at all the accumulated paperwork on his desk.

As so often happened, the line from England was clearer than from Palma. Every word the Spanish-speaking chief inspector said came through undistorted. 'About your message concerning Steven Thompson. You say that his real name was Steven Arthur Taylor and he was married to Muriel Taylor and used to live in Middle Cross, near Dover. You'll be interested to learn that, in fact, he died in a car crash in Kent roughly three years ago.'

CHAPTER 11

'I suppose,' said Superior Chief Salas, 'it is now your contention that Taylor died twice?'

'No, señor,' replied Alvarez.

'Not? But surely the idea appeals to your sense of the dramatic? And since when have you ever allowed your imagination to be constrained by impossibilities?' His anger finally surfaced. 'Goddamnit, why should I, of all people, be forced to suffer an inspector who is presented with a simple, straightforward car crash and within no more than ten days turns the incident into a second resurrection?'

'Señor, I don't see how I can be blamed for the fact that the Steven Taylor who died on this island appears also to have been the Steven Taylor who died in England.'

'Did you say "appears" to have died in England?'

'Yes . . .'

'Then you really do appreciate that it is impossible for the same man to have died twice?'

'Of course . . .'

'Experience suggests, Inspector, that in any case in which you are concerned the use of the words "of course" is irresponsible . . . In view of the fact that you accept that one or other of the reports of death must be inaccurate, what do you suggest doing?'

'We need to exhume the body of the man buried in Fogufol and Michael Taylor must be asked to identify it. If he

does identify the deceased as his father, we will know that
England made a mistake; if not, then the mistake is ours
and we will have to discover the true identity of the man
who died here.'

'Very well.'

'Shall I apply for permission for exhumation, or will you,
señor?'

'It will be best if I do. Otherwise, there's every chance
that the exhumation order will name Tutankhamen.'

A sectional ladder had been eased inside the mausoleum
and then down the shaft; two men, working with great
difficulty in the confined space, had coupled up the four
hooks of the rope sling to the coffin which had been eased
into the shaft and then hauled up by block and tackle.
Boards had been slid underneath the coffin, across the
mouth of the shaft, and it had been lowered on to these.
Four men lifted and eased it out into the open and the harsh
sunshine.

The undertaker and an assistant unscrewed the lid. The
undertaker said: 'We're ready when you are.'

Alvarez nodded.

They raised the lid. He looked down and swallowed
heavily. 'OK. Put it back on for the moment.'

He turned and walked back along the dirt track, round
the corner of the cemetery, to his parked Seat. Taylor was
standing by the passenger door. 'Are you ready?'

Taylor's face was heavy with strain; he was sweating
heavily and kept brushing the sweat away with the back of
his hand.

'Señor, it will be brief.'

'But not bloody brief enough.' He squared his shoulders.
'Let's get it over with, then.'

They walked down the dirt track to reach the coffin.
Alvarez motioned with his hand and the coffin lid was lifted
once again. Taylor stared down at the dead man for several

seconds, his face working, then he made a choking sound, turned away, and hurried over to the low drystone wall which marked the limit of the cemetery land.

Alvarez nodded and the coffin lid was replaced; the undertaker and the assistant prepared to screw it down, but he checked them. 'Hang on until I've had a word with him.'

He walked over to where Taylor stood, staring out over the land, and brought a small flask from his trouser pocket. 'This is brandy. Drink.'

Taylor took the flask, unscrewed the cap, raised the flask to his lips and drank. He passed it back.

'Was he your father?'

Taylor nodded.

'Thank you . . . I have to give one more order and then I'll drive you back.'

Taylor once more stared out, his gaze unfocused. Alvarez went back to the group of men and gave orders for the coffin to be returned to its tomb.

As Alvarez entered the guardia post on Monday morning, the duty cabo, seated behind the desk, looked up. 'There's someone waiting for you in your room; getting downright impatient. He's rung down twice to ask where the hell you've got to.'

'Who is it?'

'Borne.'

'Borne . . . Borne.' Alvarez thought for a moment, his brow furrowed. 'The name seems vaguely familiar, but I'm damned if I can think why . . .' Then a disturbing thought suddenly occurred to him. 'He's not the new comisario, is he?'

'Damned if I know, or care. But if he is your new boss, I reckon you'd better pull your finger right out.' The cabo looked at his watch. 'What time are you supposed to start work?'

'I was held up,' replied Alvarez defensively.

'Yeah. By oversleeping.'

He went up the stairs and along the corridor to his room. Inside, standing by the window, was a tall, thin man, with a long, narrow face whose sharp features expressed a strong measure of moral dyspepsia. He studied Alvarez, then said, in a voice which chilled: 'Are you the inspector?'

'Yes, señor.'

'I have been waiting here for the past twenty-two minutes. Are you not supposed to report for work by eight?'

'Indeed. And I left home well before then, but I didn't come straight here because I've an inquiry to pursue and since I couldn't find the man yesterday evening, I was hoping to do so first thing this morning.'

'You succeeded?'

'Regretfully, no. Once again, he was not at home.'

'I see.' The two words expressed disbelief, but also an acceptance of the fact that it would be almost impossible to prove Alvarez was lying. 'Hearing I had reason to come to this end of the island this morning, the superior chief suggested I spoke to you personally in the hopes that by so doing the investigation into the death of Señor Taylor might be dealt with with a little more efficiency than has hitherto been the case. When I expressed my surprise at the necessity for such a comment, he further remarked that whenever he knew you were handling a case of the slightest importance, he could never make up his mind whether he would prefer you to observe your usual level of incompetence, in which case nothing would get done, or to try to show some initiative, in which case there might well be total chaos. At the time, his words surprised me. Now they do not. Look at your desk.'

Alvarez perplexedly looked at it.

'I have never before seen such slovenly untidiness. Have you forgotten the maxim, *ex nihilo nihil fit*?'

'Er . . .'

'In future your desk will be tidy at all times and your

papers up-to-date and correctly filed. One more point; when you have occasion to pursue an investigation before reporting here in the morning, you will tell the duty guard so that he can inform anyone who inquires where you are. Is that clear?'

'Yes, señor.'

'I do not expect to have to refer to the matter again. Now, you fly to England tomorrow morning . . .'

'I what?'

'Kindly do not interrupt me. It is necessary for you to go because they stubbornly refuse to accept that it was Steven Taylor who died on this island last Wednesday week. Quite clearly, they are both unwilling and unable to accept that their own investigations of three years ago were incompetently handled. In consequence, you will now prepare a report on Taylor's death, detailing the facts in such a manner that they, despite their ludicrous pride, can no longer claim that they are right and we are wrong.' He looked at his watch. 'Thanks to your initial lateness, I am now going to have great difficulty in arriving on time for my appointment.' He walked over to the door, put his hand on the handle, stopped. 'It occurs to me that it would be best if I read through your report before you leave so that the necessary corrections can be made. Your plane takes off at eleven, which calls for you to check-in by ten . . . Be at my office at eight-thirty.'

'But . . .'

'Well?'

Alvarez realized that it would not be politic to point out that that would mean his leaving home at some quite ungodly hour. 'Nothing, señor.'

'It would clearly help you more closely to emulate *justum et tenacem propositi virum.*'

'Yes, señor.'

The comisario opened the door and left.

*

The main CID room at Brackleigh Divisional HQ was very large and it contained a dozen desks; at the far end, a space was partitioned off to form the detective-sergeant's room. Detective-Sergeant Wallace, a round, cheerful man, with the beginning of a double chin, finished reading the report which Alvarez had translated into English. He leaned back in his chair. 'I've got to admit that that seems definite. The son identified the father. So that presents us with the interesting question: Who did we bury?' He reached over for a folder and read one of the loose pages inside. 'How much do you know about our end of things?'

'Very little, señor.'

'Let's cut out this señor talk. I'm Ian and you're . . .?'

'Enrique.'

'Right . . . I'll fill you in. When your initial request about tracing the next-of-kin of Steven Thompson came in, we shunted it to the passport people. As you know, they came back with the news that the passport had been pinched some four years back. That rang the alarm bells and we asked you for further details. You then identified Steven Thompson as Steven Arthur Taylor, late of Keene House, Middle Cross. Because he'd been travelling on a stolen passport, we put his name through the computer and that came up with the information that he'd one conviction for fraud and was dead.'

He turned over a page, read for a while. 'His style of fraud wasn't original, but he was extraordinarily successful at it. I gather that basically it's a simple scheme and if the operator is very careful, not even illegal. He buys a load of shares which are quoted very low and sets out to sell them for considerably more than he paid for them. Obviously, this calls for a seller with the gift of the gab and a buyer who's either a natural sucker or else has a streak of larceny in his make-up and who, when presented with a share he's told he can buy cheaply only because someone else is being tricked into selling before discovering it's worth many times its quoted price, rushes to buy ... Taylor only ran into trouble when he let his tongue run too far ahead of the facts —drunk on his own verbosity. The judge at the trial— which was quite some time ago now—was an old fool who was gullible enough to believe Taylor's fervent promises to reform and so handed out a suspended sentence instead of sending him to jail ...

'This brings us to a little over three years ago. Word reached us that he was back to his old tricks and had overstepped the line again. We started making inquiries and eventually discovered it was true and the papers were sent to the DPP for his decision on whether to prosecute; the point at issue was, were Taylor's actions just legal or had they slipped into being illegal? It was a very abstruse point, the kind that makes a lawyer break open a celebratory bottle of champagne. Things were at that stage when he was involved in a car crash which killed him.

'Obviously, when someone under investigation has a car crash and his body is so badly burned that it is not immediately recognizable, we need to be convinced that it is his body ... What did we have here? The car was his. It had skidded off a wet road, gone through a stone parapet and crashed below, bursting into flames. The road wasn't a busy one and it was several minutes before another car came along. The driver of this raced off to the nearest house to raise the alarm and while he was away the burning car exploded.

'When it was possible, the wreck was examined. The body had fallen on to its left-hand side and because part was pressed against solid metal, we had a section of clothing and flesh which escaped burning. This gave us points to check with the wife. When he'd left the house, he'd been wearing a sports coat which she described in some detail and a blue shirt; the section of unburned coat matched her description and the shirt was blue. She told us he'd a crescent-shaped scar on his left leg, a few inches above the knee; the corpse showed signs of a crescent-shaped scar above the left knee. He'd worn dentures; we contacted his dentist who identified the dentures from the corpse as his. There was an autopsy. The deceased had not been murdered, he had died from a massive coronary thrombosis. Finally, there was not one person recently reported missing who could possibly have been the dead man.'

'That would normally seem conclusive,' said Alvarez.

'You can say that again. But now you tell us that he died in Majorca almost a fortnight ago, identified by his son, so that the corpse in the car was not his. Which raises the sixty-four thousand dollar question, how and where did he find a dead man, near enough his own age and build to be passed off as him (the evidence about the scar shows his wife was an accomplice—which in turn suggests why she sold up and left the country soon afterwards), who died a natural death and whose disappearance created no disturbance?'

'An undertaker?'

'I'd say that that's it in one. What's more, it would need to be a busy undertaker in order to provide the wide choice there would have to be for him to find a suitable candidate. And even then, it would still take time for the exact combination to turn up, which explains why he didn't fake his death when he first realized we were on to him, but waited until the last moment. He couldn't do anything else.'

They were silent for a moment, thinking about what had just been said. Wallace was the first to speak. 'I seem to remember that your report mentioned he might have been on the island on business. Was he working the same old game with the expats there?'

'I haven't been able to find out exactly what he was doing. Even his own son did not . . . That is, I believed the son when he said he did not know what his father was doing on the island, but now I begin to wonder.'

'He may have known, or guessed, but been too ashamed to speak?'

'That must be very possible. The son's relationship with his father was obviously a very stormy one, but there was still natural love. A son would always want to defend his father's reputation.'

CHAPTER 12

Brackleigh was a market town set among well-wooded countryside, some eight miles back from the coast. Not on any direct road route to London, its railway a branch line with a poor service, it had never become a commuters' town and had thereby escaped much of the sad development which had scarred so many other towns in the county.

The undertaker's premises were to the west of, and on the edge of, the town, a very convenient location since both churches were also to the west, while the crematorium was three miles further out. Wallace led the way into the reception area. A middle-aged woman asked them in a hushed voice how she could help them and Wallace said he'd like a word with Mr Gates, if free. A moment or two later, she escorted them through the Hall of Loving Care, where half a dozen coffins in different styles were tastefully on view, and into a large office.

Gates was tall, broad-shouldered, slim-waisted. He had a wide, rubbery face, an air of solicitude, and a voice with treacly undertones. He was dressed in black coat, stiff collar and black tie, and striped trousers. He shook hands with a firm, but moist grip. 'Good afternoon, gentlemen. I am delighted to make your acquaintances. Miss Carol, would you be kind enough to provide two chairs?'

She had already set one chair in front of the desk and

now she put a second one alongside it. She left, without a word.

'Miss Carol,' said Gates, as he returned round the desk and sat, 'informed me that you wished to ask me certain questions. I shall be delighted to assist in any way I can.'

'Fine,' said Wallace, who'd taken an instinctive and immediate dislike to the undertaker, but was trying not to show this. 'I think I'm right in saying that your firm conducted the funeral of Steven Arthur Taylor, of Keene House, Middle Cross, three years ago last March?'

'Who did you say?' asked Gates, inclining his head as if to hear more clearly, although previously he had shown no signs of deafness.

'Steven Arthur Taylor.'

'I do not immediately recognize the name as one of our passed-ons, but you will, I know, understand that we conduct so many laying-to-rests that it is not possible for me to remember all the names.'

'But you'll keep records?'

'Since the day this firm was founded the name of every passed-on has been recorded in the Book of Loving Remembrance.'

'Then will you check?'

Gates gestured with his plump, very white, smooth right hand. 'Naturally, I am eager to accede to your request. But will you first acquaint me with the reason for it? If you will excuse the little conceit, I regard myself as the guardian of the memories of those whose layings-at-rest I have conducted and I would not like to think that I have in any way betrayed that guardianship.'

Wallace said: 'My companion is Inspector Alvarez, from Majorca.'

'From Mallorca? . . . Please pardon my small correction, but I endeavour always to refer to a country or town in the same style as do the inhabitants; a subtle compliment to them . . . Mallorca. An island of beauty and charm. But no doubt you are well aware of its many virtues?'

'I've never been there. Inspector Alvarez has been investigating an accident in which a man died. His name was Steven Arthur Taylor.'

Gates rested his elbows on the desk, joined the tips of his fingers together to form a triangle, brushed the tips of his middle fingers backwards and forwards across the hairs which grew out of his nostrils. 'Forgive me, but I fear I have become confused. Did you not previously ask me whether we had laid to rest Mr Steven Arthur Taylor three years ago last March?'

'Yes.'

'Then I do not understand.'

'I'm wondering if you buried a man who wasn't dead.'

'Sergeant, surely you cannot begin to believe that we, or any other member of our honourable profession, could possibly lay to rest someone in whom the breath of life still lingers? Such a happening belongs only to the lowest and most disagreeable fiction.'

'That's good news for anyone in a coma, only it's not what I'm talking about. But before we go any further, suppose you check if you did handle his funeral?'

Gates, his expression pained, used the intercom to ask for the Book of Loving Remembrance to be brought in. A moment later, Miss Carol carried in a large, leather-bound ledger and carefully laid this on the desk. She left, again without a word. Gates put on a pair of spectacles and opened the ledger. After a while, he looked up. 'Steven Arthur Taylor, who had resided at Keene House, Middle Cross, was laid to rest on the sixteenth of March, three years ago.'

'Then how come he was buried a fortnight ago in Majorca?'

Gates sat back and interlocked his fingers across his lower chest. 'That is quite impossible.'

'It is what happened,' said Alvarez.

'No, señor. It cannot be what happened.'

'His body was exhumed and his son identified it.'

'Then I can only suggest . . .'

'Come off it,' said Wallace crudely. 'Where's your body buried?'

'Are you referring to Steven Arthur Taylor who passed on three years ago last March?'

'I'm referring to the man you buried, who most certainly wasn't Steven Arthur Taylor. Which cemetery is his grave in?'

'He was not laid to rest in a cemetery. His family wished him to be welcomed by the divine flame.'

'What's that mean—cremated?'

Gates inclined his head.

'How very convenient.'

'For those who do not subscribe to tradition . . .'

'For those who don't want an exhumation.'

'All the proper certificates were presented.'

'I'm sure they were.'

Gates's expression was blandly patient, but he could not quite hide the sharp watchfulness of his deep brown eyes.

'What other male funerals did you carry out during the previous week?'

'I do not think I am at liberty to answer that. As the guardian . . .'

'Then I'll get a warrant.'

Gates sighed. 'I fear, Sergeant, that you are not of a sympathetic nature.'

'In this case, you're right, I'm not. Now, do I get the names, or do I get a warrant?'

Gates leaned forward, adjusted his spectacles, read, and then slowly and reverently named ten people.

'Which of those was in his forties and died from coronary thrombosis?'

'I cannot possibly answer.'

'You must have seen the death certificates.'

'Of course. But I never record such details since when one has passed on, one's mortal . . .'

'Give me the names again, this time with the dates of the funerals. I'll check 'em out.' Wallace wrote down the list. 'Which were buried and which cremated?'

Gates provided these further details, then said very earnestly: 'Sergeant, may I ask that if you insist on disturbing their memories, that at least you conduct your inquiries with all due decorum?'

Wallace arrived at the hotel at which Alvarez was staying at six-thirty that evening and suggested they had a drink at a country pub he knew and liked. During the drive, Alvarez stared at the lush, green pastures and heavy crops and mentally compared them with those at home where, unless there was water for irrigation, pastures were burned off by the sun and crops were light. Then he stared up at the cloud-covered sky which had been threatening rain for hours and he ceased to envy the farmers whose lands promised such wealth.

The Five Legged Horse stood on crossroads, opposite what had once been the village shop, but was now a private house. The pub, reputedly an old smugglers' cottage—history, however, did not record any period of great smuggling activity in the area—had been modernized several years previously, but this had been done with taste and a happy lack of plastics, chrome, and humorous drawings.

'What'll it be, then?' asked Wallace.

Alvarez would have liked a brandy, but knew from experience that the size of an English tot would have shamed even a Basque, while its cost would be beyond disbelief.

'A lager, if they have one,' he answered, choosing to be safe.

They sat at one of the small, round tables. Wallace opened a bag of crisps and pushed this across, raised his glass. 'The first today and all the sweeter for that.' He drank, put the glass down, helped himself to a couple of crisps, munched those as he brought a sheet of paper from the breast pocket of his sports coat. 'I got one of my DCs to check out the death certificates; here's the result.'

Alvarez read down the list. 'The only real possibility is this man of forty-nine who was also cremated.'

'Right.'

'But is there any way of being certain?'

'I'd say we can be certain. The question is: Can we ever prove it? I suppose we might be able to trace out the evidence of the money Gates was paid to work the switch, but I doubt it. If you want my opinion, he's so bloody fly that only an insecticide will ever fix him.' Wallace contained a belch. 'Excuse me. Indigestion. The missus says it's because I eat too much fried food. I tell her, if the canteen didn't fry the food, we wouldn't be able to eat it.' He reached down to a pocket and brought out a small pack of tablets, one of which he swallowed. 'I've never read the instructions, in case they say, not to be taken with alcohol!'

Wallace's actions and his words recalled a scene for Alvarez. He remembered Higham's description of the meal in the restaurant up in the mountains and how Taylor had hardly drunk anything because to do so might be to trigger off the attack of migraine which the pill was meant to prevent . . . And how the subsequent violent illness had, according to himself, resembled no other attack of migraine he had ever endured . . .

'Is something up?'

'I think, Ian,' he replied slowly, 'that perhaps I have been investigating a murder without, until now, recognizing that fact.'

CHAPTER 13

'Let me try to understand,' said Superior Chief Salas wearily. 'You now claim that three years ago Steven Taylor faked his own death in England by bribing an undertaker to provide a body which he could substitute for his own in a faked car crash in order to escape arrest for fraud?'

'Yes, señor.'

'And you go on to say that Steven Taylor's real death, two weeks ago, was not accidental, but was murder—yet once again, you can prove nothing?'

'At the moment, no, but it does seem possible . . .'

'For you, is anything impossible?'

'What I've done is put two and two together . . .'

'And inevitably arrived at several solutions, none of which is four.'

Alvarez doggedly continued. 'We know that when Steven Taylor was over here, he was probably engaged in some kind of business. What could be more likely than that it was similar to what he'd done in England before his "death"—in other words, a swindling scheme? There are many wealthy foreigners who live here and by all accounts he could talk so persuasively that he could encourage even a rich man to part with money. When one swindles, one breeds bitterness and anger. Someone he swindled was determined to get his own back.'

'Did this someone arrange the car crash?'

'No, señor, what he surely did was to substitute a capsule containing poison for one containing the drug which Taylor took whenever he felt a migraine threatening. The fact that the initial symptoms of the poisoning caused him to crash was pure chance.'

'And you have reached this conclusion solely on the grounds that he was sick after the meal?'

'He ate and drank very little, then suffered symptoms that were unlike those he'd ever suffered before. Señor, I wish to investigate further.'

'How?'

'I would like to find out where he lived after his faked death and who he has defrauded on this island. May I have your permission to proceed?'

'Why bother to ask?' demanded Salas, with a fresh rush of anger. 'You never have in the past.'

Alvarez drove round the side of Las Cinco Palmeras and parked in the yard. Two cats watched him climb out of the car and then scurried away. The sun beat down and he remembered the cool, moist green of Kent.

Helen stepped out of the back door of the kitchen, hand raised to shield her eyes. When she identified her caller, her expression tightened. 'Mike's not here.'

She was a fighter, he thought admiringly. 'Do you know when he will be back, señora?'

'It's señorita and you damn well know it is.'

'I hoped you would accept that as a compliment, not as any intended insult.'

The answer surprised and bewildered her because there could be no mistaking the sincerity with which he had spoken. Then she remembered that on his previous visit he had shown himself to be very sympathetic and her manner changed. 'I'm sorry, but I really don't know when he will. You see, he's gone to try and find the builders.'

'They still have not done the work?'

She shook her head.

'Do you know their name?'

'It's Ribas. Someone told Mike that they were the most reliable people around. If they are, all I can say is, God help anyone employing one of the others.'

'I will have a word with Javier. I will tell him that if he doesn't start, I will investigate all the work he's recently done for which no proper licence was ever issued. He will arrive here immediately.'

She smiled. 'You really are a most extraordinary detective. Blackmailing a builder! You're either one of the nicest men I know, or one of the nastiest.'

'Am I permitted to ask which?'

'You may ask, but you certainly won't get an answer. Now, let's go inside and have a drink. And this time I can even offer you ice. Mike managed to persuade an electrician to come here and do a lash-up job and get one of the refrigerators running.'

They went inside. Since Alvarez's last visit, the painting had been finished and the tables and chairs were now set out. She pointed to the nearest table. 'Grab a seat. And what would you like to drink?'

She went into the kitchen, returned with a tray on which were two glasses, already frosting. 'Brandy, ice, and no soda, for you.' She handed him one glass, raised her own. 'To long, sunny days with few shadows.'

They chatted. She told him about the difficulties they had encountered in buying and altering the restaurant, trying to give it more character than it had had, and then spoke excitedly about the future.

They heard the shrill scream of the Citroën van's engine. When this was cut off, there was the slam of a door, then the stamp of approaching feet. Taylor shouted: 'Helen!'

'In the main room.'

'The bastards say . . .' He stopped abruptly as he entered and saw Alvarez. 'So it's your bloody car that's in the way.'

'Mike, the Inspector's promised to help us,' she said, trying to lessen the impact of his boorish words.

'Doing what?'

'He says he'll have a word with Ribas and persuade him to start on the work right away.'

Taylor turned and went into the kitchen. They heard the chink of ice being dropped into a glass. Helen's expression was once again worried and her previous vivacity was gone. 'Please,' she said in a low voice, 'remember it's all been so difficult for him. He's not really trying to be rude.'

Taylor returned, slumped down on the nearer of the two free chairs at the table. 'What d'you want this time—apart from free booze?'

'To tell you something and ask you something.'

'What's the news? My work permit's still at the bottom of the pile?'

'On Wednesday I flew to England and went to Brackleigh.'

Taylor's expression tightened.

'While I was there, I learned certain facts. First, your father's funeral three years ago was faked.'

'You knew that before you went.'

'Second, I learned why it was faked.'

Taylor drank, put the glass down with so much force that a few drops of liquid spurted up and spilled out on to the table. 'In this bloody world, you run and you run and still you get hit by what you're running from.'

'What d'you mean?' asked Helen, with sharp worry.

'Ask him, not me.'

She faced Alvarez. 'Why did Mike's father fake his own death?'

Alvarez hesitated.

'Are you suddenly suffering scruples?' asked Taylor violently. 'Don't bother. Have fun. Throw the family's dirty linen high into the air.'

'Señor, I would prefer to discuss the matter with you alone and then you can decide what to say to the señora.'

'D'you get an extra kick out of hypocrisy?'

'Mike!' Now there was anger as well as worry in her voice.

'What's the matter? Haven't you realized that this is other people's fun day?'

Alvarez said: 'Señor, I am here because what I have learned suggests that your father was poisoned before his death.'

'Now you're being bloody crazy.'

'Why should anyone want to poison him?' she asked.

'Because such person had been tricked out of money.'

Taylor ran his fingers through his rebellious mop of hair. He picked up his glass and drained it, abruptly stood, went through to the kitchen, returned with a bottle of brandy, one-third full, and a rubber tray of ice cubes. He sat, refilled his own glass, pushed the bottle across the table, pressed four ice cubes out of the tray into his glass. He drank heavily, then said: 'You've got to understand something. If at the beginning life hadn't kicked him so hard . . .' He stopped, slammed his clenched fist down on the table. 'Who the bloody hell am I trying to flannel? If a man's honest, he stays honest, however unfairly life treats him.'

'Can you be so sure of that?' asked Alvarez.

'What's a copper's philosophy? Call no man honest until he is dead; until then he is at best lucky? . . . Just for once, I'm going to indulge in the painful luxury of seeing things as they really are, not as I'd like them to be. Father was a man who couldn't see that there's always a distinction between right and wrong, even if the base for that distinction can shift; for him, right was what he wanted . . . I don't know what his scheme was, but it was something to do with shares. For a time, he made a lot of money and it was one of our "rich" periods, then things went wrong and he ended up in court on a charge of fraud. They found him guilty.'

She drew in her breath sharply.

He faced her. 'So now the skeleton's out of the cupboard and stalking the land and the dirty linen's flying high. If I were you, I'd start walking.'

'You damned fool,' she said, as she reached over and gripped his hand.

He drained his glass and, using his free hand, refilled it.

'D'you want to learn what hell really is? It's not the traditional pit of flames, it's not merely Sartre's other people, it's a crowd of little bastards of your own age circling you and shouting that your father's a thief. D'you want to know what abject, humiliating betrayal is? It's standing in the middle of that circle and hating your father and wishing to God you could be given the chance of denying him . . .

'He was sentenced two days after he was found guilty. The judge said he'd needed that time to consider the matter. He decided not to jail Father because he saw in him a sense of real remorse and the desire for redemption . . . I can still remember Father laughing and boasting about how he'd softened up the old fool of a judge with his superb eloquence; laughing, when I'd been suffering hell because of him . . . We left that district, which meant I changed schools. No one ever found out at the new one what had happened and for once some of the boys were friendly to me even though I was a newcomer, arriving in the middle of the term. So life ought to have been a whole lot happier. But every time I looked at Father, I remembered how I'd have denied him if only I'd been given the opportunity . . .

'Then he met Muriel. As I said, he saw things not as they were, but as he wanted them to be. Before he married her, he saw her as a loving wife whose money would screen him from ever again risking imprisonment. He couldn't see her as the bitch she really was.

'There was never any mistaking his background, even though he never tried to impress; even when he stepped out of the dock a convicted, but freed, criminal, he was one of the upper crust. And when they were together, this became even more obvious; as did the fact that her background was totally different. And because she's an arrant snob, she pretty soon came to hate him for something over which he'd no control. And d'you know how she set out to get her own back? By making him plead with her for every penny she gave him. Then, she could despise him.

'I couldn't stand seeing him humiliated, so I cleared out. Just before I went, I told him he'd got to do the same. He laughed and said he would, all in good time. I soon learned what that really meant. He'd worked out a new scheme for making money and was determined to get this going and so become financially independent before he broke away from her. I told him to forget it—look at last time. He said it wasn't the same and the idea was cast-iron. Soft brass, more like. Things went wrong and the police got on his trail again and it became clear that the moment they'd collected enough evidence, they'd arrest him for fraud. And this time, not even he could be bloody optimistic enough to believe the judge would give him a second chance. It would be jail. And so he thought up a way of escape. And because, with his help, she'd been impersonating the landed gentry—large house and God knows how many acres, cherry brandy stirrup cup for the hunt—the thought of what people would say if he was publicly branded a convicted criminal was enough to give her hysterics. She agreed to finance his plan.'

There was a long silence, which Alvarez broke. 'Thank you for telling me all that.'

Taylor shrugged his broad shoulders.

'Where has your father been living in the past three years?'

'I don't know.'

'You really do not have any idea?'

'Look, I cleared out because I couldn't stand what was going on. It was a complete break.'

'When you saw him here, he didn't mention anywhere?'

'Not specifically. But on one occasion he talked about getting the train into Barcelona, so I suppose if he had a place, it was near there.'

'How near?'

'I've told you all he ever said; and if he'd ever said any more, I bloody wouldn't pass it on.'

'Why not?'

'Haven't you understood what I've been saying?'

'Yes, señor, I have. But have you, for your part, under-stood that if he was murdered, it is necessary to find the murderer? Can you tell me whether he was carrying out some business on this island?'

'No, I can't.' He poured himself a third drink. 'All right, you'd have to be stupid not to be able to guess. He'd some scheme or other going on.'

'A scheme that was connected with shares?'

'What d'you think?' Taylor stared into space. 'And you know something really comic? He'd finally hit the jackpot. He told me that when he gave us the money to buy this place. He'd made so much that he was going to retire and imitate an honest man. He'd made it, just in time to die . . . according to you, to be murdered.'

He'd been murdered, thought Alvarez, because he had been about to retire a dishonest man, not an honest one.

Alvarez stared at the list of figures which the meteorological office in Palma had just provided over the telephone. On May 14 Steven Taylor had flown in to Mallorca and that day the weather had, along the Mediterranean coast, been sharply layered as it often was at that time of the year. From the French border to just south of Barcelona, there had been strong winds and the temperature had been cool (relatively speaking); from just south of Barcelona to Alicante, the winds had been light and the temperature warm; further south still, there had been virtually no wind and the tem-perature had been hot. These conditions had been holding for several days. Taylor had told the man in Worldwide Car Hire, at Palma airport, that he had just come from somewhere noticeably colder; he had told the porter at Hotel Verde that recently there had been too much wind for him to sail his boat; he had told his son that he had caught a train to Barcelona. Put those facts together and there was good reason for saying that he had been living on the coast between Barcelona and the French border.

It was going to be necessary to telephone Salas. Alvarez sighed, leaned over and opened the bottom right-hand drawer of his desk. He brought out the bottle of brandy and a glass.

CHAPTER 14

The moving walkway carried Alvarez from the airport to the station, from which a train left within five minutes. On arrival at Sants, the more westerly of Barcelona's stations, he inquired when the next train for Figueras left, and from which station, and was told that the TALGO would be departing from there in twenty minutes.

He enjoyed train travel. One didn't take off and land, so that there was no need to shut one's eyes and pray, believing, yet very conscious that there were times when the Almighty slipped up. He stared out at the green, rolling, and in parts wooded countryside, and thought that here one could buy very many more hectares of fertile land for the same money as on the island. Perhaps after he'd retired, he could move to the Peninsula and buy the finca he had always longed to own, could till the land, plant the seed, harvest the crop . . . But he knew he was deceiving himself. He would never be truly happy away from the island.

The train drew into Figueras and he alighted. He'd been promised that someone from the municipal police would meet him, but there was not a uniform in sight so he crossed to a seat, near a board which showed the make-up of the next train to Barcelona, and let the drowsy warmth engulf him . . .

'Inspector Alvarez?'

He awoke with a jerk, stood, and shook hands with a man much younger than himself who spoke in Catalán, yet seemed to have some difficulty in understanding his Mallorquín. They walked down the platform and left by one of the unmanned exits, crossed to a car which was parked under the shade of a tree. They drove to the police HQ, an old four-storey building not far from the Dalí museum. There, he spoke to a man who had checked with the town hall and the Ministry of the Interior. 'Sorry, but there's no house been purchased by a Steven Arthur Thompson and no one of that name's taken out a residencia or permanencia.'

'Blast!'

'Don't forget, despite the amnesty, there are still one hell of a lot of foreigners living in the area who ought to have papers, but don't.'

'You wouldn't have a list of 'em?'

The man laughed. 'I don't know exactly what you had in mind . . .?'

He looked at his watch. 'A drink and then lunch.'

Along the coast, a number of developments specifically aimed at yachtsmen had been built and of these, Corleon, set around canals, was perhaps the best. Spain's answer to Port Grimaud. Unfortunately, its initial success had proved to be far in excess of expectations, with predictable results. More canals were dredged, the density of housing was increased and finally, on the outskirts of the urbanización, dozens of rabbit hutches were built, specifically aimed at the French holiday market, while large and ugly blocks of appartments began to line the beach.

Alvarez parked the borrowed car and climbed out. The sun shone out of a cloudless sky, but a sea breeze prevented the heat from building up. He looked across the raised pavement at the estate agent and sighed. When he'd said that he intended questioning all the estate agents in Corleon to find out if any one of them had sold a house to Steven Thompson, which for some reason had not been registered, he had been regarded with amusement. Having gained a rough idea of the number of estate agents there were, he understood the reason for that amusement.

Two hours later, he used a handkerchief to wipe the sweat from his forehead and neck; it might not be as hot as on the island, but it was still too warm to spend the day walking from one office to another, asking the same questions, receiving the same answers . . . And if he failed to find any trace of Steven Thompson here, there were many more developments up and down the coast . . . Across the wide road was a café, with tables and chairs set outside under the shade of an awning. He waited for a French registered Mercedes to drive past at twice the speed that was reasonable, crossed and gratefully sat. He ordered a coffee and coñac.

Had he made too many assumptions, he wondered, as he drank and watched with appreciation the scantily clad women go by—it was difficult to remember that there'd been a time when even men in bathing trunks had been supposed to wear guards over their knees. When told that Steven Taylor enjoyed sailing and owned a boat, he'd assumed this to be a sailing boat which probably required a berth; but 'sailing' could mean a power boat, which could be moved by trailer so that Taylor might well live inland. He'd assumed . . . A young lady, wearing a see-through blouse and no brassière, went past and the sharp sunlight picked out the curves of her flesh. He watched her cross to the far side of the road and enter a large supermarket. That gave him an idea.

He finished the coffee and coñac, paid the bill, which was high enough to make it clear that few locals ever drank there, left and crossed the road to the supermarket. He asked the cashier at the one till which was operating if the owner was around and she answered that if Agueda wasn't downstairs, she'd be upstairs, in tones which suggested that Agueda kept a suspicious eye on everything at all times.

Agueda was checking through a display of beach accessories.

'From Llueso? My mother was born not ten kilometres from there and many's the time I've been there before I was married! Tell me, how much has it changed?' She was a large, heavily-boned woman who deliberately dressed to emphasize her size rather than to conceal it. She used a great deal of make-up and her mouth was a most unusual colour. She wore so much jewellery that most people assumed it to be imitation, but in fact it was all genuine.

They went down to the ground floor and through to the office which lay behind the bread counter. She offered him a drink. 'Well, what is it you want exactly?' she asked, as she handed him two glasses and a bottle.

'I'm trying to find out more about a foreigner who died on the island recently; I don't have an address, but there's reason to believe he lived here.'

'You must have asked at the town hall in Figueras?'

'I have, but no luck; and the same goes for the estate agents. So I'm wondering if he rents a place, in which case it could prove difficult to track him down. But I reckoned there's just the chance you could have come across him.'

'Most of the foreigners come here to shop,' she agreed complacently, fingering one of her rings as she spoke. 'What's the name?'

'Steven Thompson.'

She repeated the names, her heavy accent distorting them. She shook her head. 'I don't know anyone by that name.'

'Ah well, it was just an off-chance,' he said philosophically. 'Tomorrow morning, I'll see if any of the banks have changed money for him.'

'Here, fill your glass again. But leave mine as it is.'

He gave himself a generous drink, happy to make the most of the chance to enjoy the Carlos I brandy.

'What was that first name again?'

'Steven. It's possible it was usually shortened to Steve.'

'Steve . . . Steve . . . I've heard that before. I wonder if . . . When did this man die?'

'A fortnight ago last Wednesday.'

'You know, that could be about the time.'

'What could?'

'When the woman lost her man.' She continued with all the enthusiasm and irrelevancies of a born gossip. Charlotte Benbury was always called Charlie, which was confusing because an Englishman had told her that Charlie was a man's name. Still, when one stopped to think about it, Spain wasn't always that logical. A man was called José-María, but María was a woman's name. And it was better to be called a woman's name than Jesus. Agueda snorted. As a good communist—as she gesticulated to emphasize her standing, one of the diamonds on the largest ring caught the light and flashed out ice-cold sparks of colour—she had only contempt for people so conditioned by superstition . . . To get back to Charlie? Well, she was English. And men clearly found her very attractive. But then any man under the age of ninety was interested in only one thing, so none of them could see that she was a bitch . . .

'Why d'you say that?' he asked.

'Because that's what she is.'

She wasn't a prude by any means, but there were limits. When Charlie's man had been alive, they'd been like a honeymoon couple, even though he was a good bit older than she. Then he'd died and what had happened? Had she mourned her lost love? Had she hell! Within something like three days, she'd reappeared and started going about with Pierre, the Frenchman, who boasted that during the summer season he never bedded the same woman two nights running. When the two of them had walked into the supermarket, arms about each other's waists, she'd wondered why God —not that she believed in such a superstition—had not struck her dead.

'What happened to the first man?'

'Someone said he'd been killed in a car crash.'

'D'you know where?'

'Can't say. And if you want my opinion, it's a great pity she wasn't with him at the time.'

'The young do things differently these days,' he said pacifically.

'The men don't,' she replied with crushing contempt.

'Is she still living here?'

'I saw her only yesterday. The bitch.'

There was possibly, he thought, more than a touch of jealousy in her outrage; perhaps her youth had been conventionally dull. 'D'you know where she lives?'

'Somewhere in Servas. I don't know the number, but it's the biggest house around, on the water, and there's a huge yacht tied up. Masses of money. D'you think she'll get all that?'

'How would I know?'

'It'd be just like a fool man to have left her everything so that now she can waste it on that Pierre.'

'Lucky Pierre.'

She was not amused.

He found the house quite easily. It was a long U-shaped bungalow, built on two plots, and it fronted one of the main canals so that a yacht, fully rigged, could berth there. To the left was a hard tennis court and to the right a swimming pool, partially concealed from the road by a row of cupressus. The property was ringed by a high chain-link fence and both the small and the large gates were secured with heavy locks. At regular intervals there was a notice which said in Spanish, English, and German, that the house was protected by alarms and guard dogs.

He pressed the button of the speaker, to the side of the smaller gate. 'Who is it?' asked a woman in Catalán, her voice sounding harsh and tinny.

He identified himself and said he'd like a word with the señorita.

'You can come on in; the dog's shut up in the kennel.' There was a sharp click from the lock of the gate.

As he walked through the gateway, a dog began to bark and he saw to the side of the house an enclosure in which, standing very stiff-legged, was a large, woolly, black dog whose teeth, even at a distance, struck him as exceedingly dangerous.

A middle-aged woman in an apron opened the front door and showed him into a very large sitting-room, tastefully furnished with good quality Spanish furniture; through one of the picture windows, he could look across the sloping garden to a schooner. Money might not buy happiness, but it helped one to enjoy one's misery . . .

'Good evening. You wish to speak?' asked a woman in laboured Castilian.

He turned. Agueda had referred to Charlotte Benbury as being very attractive, but she had also named her bitch so that he had subconsciously been expecting her character to flavour her looks. Far from it. She was of such pure, stunning beauty that for a moment she shocked; tall, shapely, a round face topped by a cascade of honey-coloured hair, eyes more blue than the summer Mediterranean, a mouth shaped by Cupid, peaches-and-double-cream complexion . . . He saw both innocence and experience, cool purity and fervid passion . . . 'I am sorry, I was admiring the yacht,' he said in English, trying to explain away his gaucherie. 'May I have a word with you?'

'Thank goodness, you speak English!' She smiled.

A man would run ten miles in the July heat for such a smile . . . 'Señorita, as your maid probably told you, I have very recently arrived from Mallorca where I have been investigating the death of Señor Thompson, whose real name was Taylor.'

She bit her lower lip, hesitated, moved to her right to sit in an armchair.

'You knew him?'

She nodded.

'He lived here?'

She nodded again.

'I am sorry to have to pursue a subject which must be painful—' Perhaps!—'but because of certain facts surrounding his death, I must. You will have been told that he was in a car which crashed; did you also know that his passenger was lucky enough to be thrown clear before the car reached the bottom of the cliff and so lived?'

'All I care is that Steve was killed.' Her tone was flat, her expression blank.

'The passenger suffered some injuries and for a while lost his memory. When this returned, he told us certain facts which have subsequently raised very serious questions.'

She was staring into the far distance, almost as if bored.

He spoke more starkly than he would otherwise have done, determined to force her to understand that the past could not be as readily dismissed as she would have it. 'What the passenger told us makes it seem certain that the crash occurred because Señor Taylor had been poisoned.'

'What?' She swung round to face him, her expression now strained. 'That's impossible.'

'It is the truth.'

She began to pluck at a fold in her linen print frock.

'Did the señor suffer from migraine attacks?'

'Yes.'

'Did he know when an attack was impending?'

'Sometimes. Not always.' She spoke in a nervous, staccato manner.

'Have you any idea what triggered an attack?'

'Chocolate, cheese.'

'What about wine?'

'He thought it did. But he liked it so much . . .' She failed to finish the sentence.

'What did he do if he believed an attack was starting?'

'He'd take medicine.'

'Would there be any of it in this house?'

'Maybe.'

'You've been too busy with other matters to discover what he's left?' he said, which heavy sarcasm.

She looked at him with sudden alarm. So, he thought, she wasn't completely indifferent to other people's opinions. 'Did you know that Señor Thompson's real name was Taylor?'

She made no reply.

'Did you?'

'Yes.'

'Do you know why he lived under a false name?'

'What's it matter now?'

'Because it probably explains why he was poisoned. Did he ever tell you he'd faked his own death in England in order to escape being arrested for fraud?'

After a while, she nodded.

'That fraud was in connection with share dealings. Since he lived here, did he deal in shares?'

'I . . .' She stopped.

'Do you want to help, or don't you? Does it matter at all to you that he was poisoned?'

'Of course it does.'

'Then had he been dealing in shares?'

'Yes.'

'How?'

'I don't know. I asked him once what it was he was doing and he refused to explain. He said it was much safer for me not to know.'

'Didn't you ever gain any hint?'

'No.'

'It's almost impossible to run any kind of a business without records. Did he keep them?'

'I suppose so.'

'Why are you uncertain?'

'He often used to work in the study, but if I went in there I never looked at what he was doing.'

'Are you saying you weren't in the least bit curious?'

'He was insistent that I never learned anything.'

'Because if something went wrong, you wouldn't be inculpated?'

'Yes.'

And you repay his love by offering yourself to Pierre only days after his death, he wanted to say, but didn't. Are all his papers still in the study?'

'I haven't touched anything.'

'Then I want your permission to look through them.'

For a while she made no comment, then she stood and it was obvious that this was the answer.

The large room was both library and study. Two of the walls were lined with shelves filled with books, there was a small desk, and an old-fashioned, free-standing safe.

The drawers of the desk contained nothing of interest. He asked her for the keys of the safe and she left, returned with them. On the top shelf of the safe there was a jewellery case and a considerable amount of money in pounds, dollars, and pesetas; on the bottom shelf were several files. He lifted out the files and put them on the desk.

It soon became obvious that Steven Taylor had been a systematic man. Each file covered a geographical region and one was for Mallorca. This contained papers listing the names and addresses of Archie Wheeldon/Muriel Taylor, Robert Reading-Smith, and Valerie Swinnerton. Against each name was a figure, two hundred thousand, four hundred thousand, forty thousand and a company's name.

'Do you know what Yabra Consolidated is?'

She shook her head.

'Would you know if Señor Taylor left a will?'

'Yes, he did.'

'Where is it?'

'In one of the files.'

He looked through those he had not examined and found two wills, one in Spanish, one in English, that were essentially the same. Taylor had named only one beneficiary, his son.

'Do you know the terms of his wills?'

She nodded.

'You're not mentioned. So his son now owns this house and all its contents.'

'No. Steve bought it in my name. That's why I put it up for sale, not him.'

'When was this?'

'I don't know. Maybe a couple of months ago.'

'Why are you trying to sell?'

'Steve told me to.'

'What was his reason for wanting to move?'

'He was worried?'

'About what?'

'Someone had threatened him.'

'Who?'

'He wouldn't say.'

'Have you any idea how much his son stands to inherit?'

'No.'

'Where is his money held?'

'I don't know.'

'You must.'

'I don't. I've an account with the Banque de Crédit Agricole in Berne and he paid money into that when it was needed. He never said where that money came from.'

'Then how will his son learn the extent of his inheritance?'

'I suppose he's told Mike where he kept his capital.'

'You've met Mike?'

'No. But Steve often talked about him.'

He checked through all the files again, seeking a reference to bank accounts, but there was none. He replaced the files in the safe, locked it, handed her the keys. 'Where will I find the medicine?'

She led the way into a bedroom that was nearly as large as the sitting-room and also faced the canal. The furniture was a strangely harmonious mixture of modern and antique so that the Spanish bed with barley-sugar headboard and footboard did not seem at all out of place in company with the superbly inlaid, serpentine dressing-table whose delicate elegance suggested it was French. To the side of a heart-shaped mirror on the dressing-table was a framed photograph. It was a poor photograph because flat lighting had stripped away all subtlety; nevertheless it was possible to discern in it all the features of the dead man he had seen in the coffin, even though many of those features had been attacked by decay. The frame was antique embossed silver. How, he wondered, could she leave that photograph there when she shared the bed with Pierre?

She opened the small top left-hand drawer of the dressing-table and brought out a medicine bottle and handed this to him. He unscrewed the lid. Inside were a number of capsules, half red and half white. 'I'd like to take these.'

'I don't want them.'

He pocketed the bottle. He was glad that now he could leave.

As he sat behind the wheel of his car, he saw that she was still standing in the front doorway of the house. What were her real emotions? Worry and shame, not because of what she'd done, but because he might have learned of what she'd done? He knew a sudden, sharp anger that anyone so beautiful could at heart be so rotten . . . But that, surely, was to ignore completely the question of what kind of a man Taylor had been? Might he not have been swindling her out of love, as he had swindled others out of money? Might she not have discovered this and that was why she had been so ready to throw herself into the arms of another man? . . . Yet if that were so, could she really have been so hypocritical as to keep the photo on the dressing-table instead of ripping it out of the frame? He swore. He knew precisely what he was doing. Searching for what was not there because he was far too sentimental; inventing the most ridiculous excuses rather than admit that there could be evil in beauty.

CHAPTER 15

Alvarez sat in his office and stared through the window. The day was already pulsatingly hot; there had been no rain for weeks and wells were beginning to empty and in another month only those which tapped underground streams or lakes would not be dry; on unirrigated land, all growth would shrivel to a uniform brown and it would seem as if the earth itself were dying . . .

Reluctantly, he jerked his thoughts back to the present and for a while he considered all the work he should be doing. Then he rang the Institute of Forensic Anatomy and spoke to Professor Fortunato's secretary. Were the results of the post mortem on Señor Steven Taylor yet to hand? Frostily, she replied that since the exhumation had taken place as recently as the previous Saturday morning, they were hardly likely to be.

He telephoned Detective-Sergeant Wallace at Divisional HQ in Brackleigh. Was Yabra Consolidated the name of shares and, if it was, what were they worth?

'You must have a funny idea of the kind of money we make, Enrique, to ask me! The only thing I can tell you about shares is, they're dangerous. A mate of mine decided to go for British Telecom and when they started to rise his wife persuaded him to sell because she wanted a new settee.

After he'd sold 'em they continued to rise and she went for him all ends up for losing so much money by selling. Nearly caused a divorce, that did!'

'But you perhaps know someone who can tell me the answers?'

'Sure. A mate works for a stockbroker in the City and his bonus each year almost makes my entire salary look silly. I'll chat him up and then get back on to you. By the way, what's the weather like?'

'Sunny and much too hot.'

'It's stair-rodding here and bloody cold. Can't you dig up a case that needs me along to give a hand?'

After saying goodbye, Alvarez slumped back in the chair. Apart from sending the capsules he had brought back from Corleon to Palma for testing, there really was nothing more he could do. Nothing more, that was, other than to make a start on clearing up the backlog of work on his desk . . .

'You're looking tired,' said Dolores, as she looked across the luncheon table at Alvarez.

'And old,' said Juan. Isabel giggled.

She swung round. 'How dare you say such a thing!'

'But he's becoming bald.'

'Another word from you and I'll wash your mouth out with kitchen soap.'

Juan felt aggrieved because he had only spoken the truth, and all his life he'd been instructed to do that, but he knew better than to argue with his mother when her voice held that sharp tone.

'You can go outside and play,' she said.

He reluctantly stood—he was certain the grown-ups were going to talk about something interesting—and left, followed by his sister.

'You're looking tired,' said Dolores, for the second time.

Alvarez ran his forefinger along the line of his hair and persuaded himself that it had not receded.

'You need a really good siesta.'

Jaime passed the bottle of brandy across. 'This'll help you sleep.'

Dolores pursed her lips, but for once kept quiet. After all, her husband might just be right.

Alvarez drank the last of the coffee, checked the time. 'I'd better be moving.'

Dolores, already beginning to prepare the supper, looked up from the chopping-board. 'Be back on time. I'm making frito Mallorquín.'

'I'll be back before time,' he promised. Her frito Mallorquín was the best on the island. Not a trace of greasiness.

He left the house, drove to the main square, and was lucky enough to find a newly vacated parking space against the central, raised portion. Practically all the tables set out in front of the two cafés were occupied. The tourists would be paying one price for their drinks, the foreign residents less, and Mallorquins, if any, less still. Which was just. Let the visitors pay for at least some of the damage they caused . . .

He walked down one of the narrow roads and reached the guardia building, went up to his room and sat, waiting to phone until he'd regained his breath.

Wallace spoke with cheerful surprise. 'You've pulled a right one out of the bag this time, Enrique!'

'I'm afraid I don't quite understand.'

'Then pin back your ears and prepare to listen to a modern fairy story . . . When you first mentioned Yabra Consolidated, the name seemed to ring a bell, but I was damned if I could think why. Then this pal of mine who works in a stockbroker's office told me what's what and I remembered all the press hullabaloo. Yabra Consolidated is the name of an Australian mining company. The Australians are great gamblers and one of the things which really attracts the punters is stocks and shares. Not surprisingly, this brings the worms out of the woodwork and they set up very doubtful, or downright bogus, companies, flog the shares and get rich, leave the punters to become poor. The mining sector's the worst. There've been three companies in the past twelve months who've been caught salting land or faking assays to promote a good launch of shares.

'Yabra Consolidated was formed five years ago to prospect for gold, uranium, and diamonds. As my pal said, that combination of aims would have taxed even a large and established company and so it ought to have warned the punters, but it didn't. The shares were fully subscribed at a dollar each. A year ago, they stood at two cents and that, apparently, was an overvaluation.

'Then, recently, the impossible happened. Gold was discovered on land over which the company has mineral rights and the shares shot up and up until right now they're standing at five dollars.'

'But that's . . .' Alvarez stopped.

'Yeah, I know. Backside about face.'

'I was sure Taylor had persuaded people to pay money for shares he knew to be worthless. Instead of which . . .'

'Instead of which, it sounds as if he was hoist with his own petard.' Wallace chuckled. 'Can you imagine his feelings when he discovered that instead of swindling his victims, he'd made them rich?'

'But from all accounts, he had made a great deal of money for himself shortly before he died.'

'Then either he talked himself into keeping some of the shares or else he heard they'd unexpectedly come good and he was in time to buy them back before the news became general.'

And that, thought Alvarez, would be quite enough to make a seller think of murder. He started to thank the other, when Wallace checked him.

'Hang on. There's another piece of news which should interest you. One of my blokes has told me that not very long ago he had a private detective try to pump him about Steven Taylor.'

'In what connection?'

'It wasn't all that clear, but it seemed as if this man had been employed to discover if Taylor had any sort of a record.'

'Why should he have been suspected?'

'I can't answer. If you're interested, I'll find out as much as I can.'

'Will you? And especially the client's name.'

'Leave it with me . . . By the way, how's the weather now?'

'Still too hot.'

'We haven't seen the sun in days. Why in hell can't you be having rain just once when I'm talking to you?'

The chemist shop was in the same narrow road as the guardia post, but nearer to the square. A married couple, both of whom were qualified pharmacists, ran it and Alvarez went through and spoke to the husband who was checking stock in the room beyond the shop.

'So how are things with you?' asked the husband.

'I can't complain.'

'Then you're the only one who can't, with IVA doubling prices . . . Francisca saw Dolores the other day and said she thought Dolores wasn't looking too fit; could that be right?'

For a while, they spoke about general matters of interest. Although about ten thousand people lived in and around Llueso, so few of them or their ancestors had ever lived anywhere else that relationships were extensive and complex. It was relatively rare for two locals to meet and not to have at least one distant cousin in common. Finally, Alvarez brought the conversation round to the reason for his present visit. He produced the medicine bottle Charlotte had given him. 'What can you tell me about the contents?'

'Is this an official question?'

'At the moment it's unofficial, but it's likely to go official very soon.'

'Have you any idea what the capsules are for?'

'They're said to be for an impending migraine attack.'

The husband crossed to a small desk, brought down three fat books from a shelf, searched through these, frequently referring back to the capsules. At the end of five minutes, he said: 'As far as I can tell, they're what the label says they are. Of course, it'll take an analysis to be certain, but on visual identification these capsules contain a drug that is put out for migraine sufferers to help ward off attacks.'

'How long would one take to work after swallowing?'

'I don't know that I'd like to say—you'll have to ask the manufacturer. All that's certain is that they'll be fairly fast because if they're to stop an attack consolidating, they've got to be.'

'Something like a quarter of an hour?'

'I doubt it's that quick, but as I said, you'll have to ask the manufacturer.'

Taylor had taken one capsule earlier in the morning and then a second one just before—or was it with?—the meal at the restaurant because the first one hadn't worked. It looked, then, as if it was probably the earlier one which had contained the poison. 'Would it be difficult to substitute a foreign substance for the drug in one of the capsules?'

'Nothing easier. They're made in halves. All you'd have to do would be to separate the two, empty out the contents and put in whatever you wanted . . . Are you saying that that's what was done?'

'It looks like it.'

'So then what happened?'

'The driver of a car crashed and was killed.'

The husband whistled.

CHAPTER 16

El Granero was a part of the island which Alvarez seldom visited. First, it lay to the west of Palma, near concrete-jungle land, secondly, it was a development unashamedly pitched at the rich, thirdly and most importantly, Granero meant granary, a name which reached back to the time when one half of the island's grain had been grown there, and the contrast between past and present was too bitter.

He drove past houses set in large gardens which raised his scorn for so much wasted land, came in sight of Ca'n Grande and suddenly all scorn was gone and he knew only a wistful wonder that anyone could be so lucky as to own and live in anywhere so beautiful. The rock, suddenly breaking out of the rich soil, stretched out into the small bay and the house seemed to flow upwards from the rock, as if built by nature, not man.

It grew in size as he approached, not simply because he was nearer to it, but because the graceful lines helped to conceal until the last moment exactly how large it was. He parked, by the side of a bed filled with magnificent roses in full bloom, and walked up to the heavy wooden door which had the deep rich patina which came only from regular hard polishing. He rang the bell and the maid answered it, then led him through a hall and a wide passage out on to the patio. She said she'd call the señora.

He looked out at the sea, spread below, and he thought that here was somewhere which rivalled even his beloved Llueso bay . . .

'You wish to speak to me?'

He turned and saw a woman who almost managed to conceal her age with elegance; her expression and tone of voice denoted bored indifference. 'Yes, señora.'

'In what connection?'

'Señor Taylor.'

'I fail to see that the subject of my late husband can be of any concern to you.'

'Not even,' he said, choosing to be objectionable, 'when he died twice?'

She walked over to the swing chair and settled in the shade of the awning.

He moved a chair and sat. 'Your husband was supposed to have died three years ago, in England, but in fact he died here, on this island, almost three weeks ago.'

She gave no indication that she had heard him.

'Can you tell me what he was doing on this island?'

'No, I cannot.'

'Then full inquiries into his supposed death will have to be made in England; how he faked it, whom he bribed, and where the money for that bribe came from.'

'Are you trying to blackmail me?'

'Señora, I am a member of the Cuerpo General de Policía.'

'What's the significance of that? You're asking twice as much?'

'The suggestion is insulting.'

The lift of her eyebrows suggested that she was surprised he believed himself capable of being insulted.

He struggled to keep his temper in check as he thought that it was small wonder the British had been booted out of their Empire. 'Did you see your husband three weeks ago?'

'I did not.'

'Are you quite certain?'

'I am not in the habit of lying. Or, I might add, of being called a liar.'

'Can you explain why your name and address were written down in one of his business files?'

'I wouldn't bother to try.'

'I believe it was because in the last few months he sold you certain shares.'

'If you can believe that, you can believe anything.'

'Did you buy shares from him?'

'I have already indicated that I most certainly did not.'

'Did he offer to sell you some?'

'He was not that much of a fool.'

The maid stepped out on to the patio. 'Señor Wheeldon, señora.'

'You can ask him to come through.' She turned back to Alvarez. 'Is there anything more before you go?'

'Yes, señora.'

'How very boring.' She looked towards the house and as Wheeldon appeared, she called out: 'Archie, will you tell Catalina to bring out the drinks trolley?'

Wheeldon briefly returned into the house, then crossed the patio. ''Morning, Muriel.' He looked at Alvarez as he waited for the introduction.

'He's from the police.'

'The police, eh?' Wheeldon looked round for a patio chair, brought one across. He grinned as he sat. 'What have you been up to, old girl? Robbing a bank?'

'Don't be so bloody stupid.'

'Here, I was only having a little joke.'

'That's all I need to make my day!'

'You mean something really is wrong?'

'Señor,' said Alvarez, 'I am investigating the circumstances of Señor Steven Taylor's death.'

'But he died three years back, in England. What's that to do with you now?'

'Señor Taylor died three weeks ago, on this island.'

Wheeldon said to Muriel: 'I say, what the devil's he getting at? You've told me yourself that your husband died before you came out here.'

She said, with cold fury: 'He was Steven Thompson.'

He stared at her, slack-jawed. 'But you said . . .'

'Will you stop saying the same thing over and over again. The English police made a mistake in identification.'

'But . . . but dammit, you must have discovered that he wasn't really dead?' Only after he'd finished speaking did he realize the implications of what he'd just said.

The maid, wheeling a cocktail trolley, came out on to the patio. She positioned it close to Muriel's chair and checked that the brake was on. 'Is some crisps, señora. 'And . . .'

'That's all.'

The maid returned into the house.

'I want a whisky,' Muriel said.

Wheeldon stood, opened the two top flaps of the trolley and these, through a system of counterweights, brought up a shelf on which were several bottles, an insulated ice container, and half a dozen glasses. He poured out a whisky on the rocks and passed her the glass. He looked at Alvarez. 'He doesn't want anything,' Muriel said. Innate courtesy made him ask Alvarez: 'Are you quite certain you won't have something?'

'Thank you, I'd like a coñac, please, with ice but no soda.'

She became still angrier.

Wheeldon poured himself a pink gin, sat.

'Señor,' said Alvarez, 'did you meet Señor Thompson, or Taylor, when he was on this island?'

Wheeldon cleared his throat. 'As a matter of fact, I did, yes.'

'Where did this happen?'

'At some party or other; I can't remember exactly which.'

'And when was this?'

'The first time? I suppose it was three or four months ago.'

'You've seen him since then?'

'I . . . Well, as a matter of fact, I have, yes.'

'You saw him again?' she said sharply.

'Look, I'd no idea he was your husband. You never said anything.'

'Of course I damn well didn't.'

'But why not?'

'God Almighty, that has to be the year's stupidest question.'

'Señor,' said Alvarez, 'did you buy shares from him?'

She said, her voice filled with scorn: 'Not even Archie could be that soft.'

Wheeldon spoke uneasily. 'I . . . The thing is . . .'

'Christ! You're not trying to say you actually did?'

'He made it sound so promising.'

'Of course he did. And you believed him? It's a wonder he didn't sell you a slice of moon cheese at the same time.'

'I'm not quite as thick as you seem to think.'

'Impossible.'

'I doubled my money.'

She laughed scornfully.

'I'm telling you, I literally doubled my money. What's more, if you like I can prove it.' He stood, crossed to the cocktail trolley and poured himself a second pink gin.

'How much did you pay for the shares, señor?' Alvarez asked.

'It was the equivalent of five cents, Australian,' he answered, as he sat.

'How many did you buy?'

'Two hundred thousand.'

'And what did you sell them for?'

'Ten cents clear.'

'You made ten thousand Australian dollars?' she said, her voice high from astonishment.

'Yes, I did.'

'Señor,' said Alvarez, 'how much would your holding be worth now?'

Wheeldon picked up his glass and drank quickly.

Muriel looked at Alvarez, then at Wheeldon. 'How much, Archie?'

'I don't know.'

'What's the name of the shares?'

'I've forgotten.'

'Yabra Consolidated,' said Alvarez.

'What? You bought Yabra Consolidated at five cents?'

'Yes.'

'And then sold them at ten? When they're now worth over five dollars?'

'How was I to know . . .?'

'D'you realize how much you've lost?'

'I haven't lost anything. I told you, I've doubled my money.'

'Christ! you've got a mind that walks one inch high. Your holding's now worth a million dollars. But you sold it for ten thousand. You gave him practically a million!'

'I didn't give him anything. He bought them from me . . .'

'You call it buying, when he knew they were worth fifty times what he was paying for them?'

'Maybe he didn't.'

'You can really think he'd offer you a profit if he didn't know they were worth five dollars? My late husband may have been many things, but he was nobody's fool. He'd sized you up as God's gift to a con-man from the moment he first met you. Don't you have the wit to understand anything? When you bought those shares at five cents, they wouldn't have been worth half that. Then they shot up and he must have been absolutely shocked to discover that for once in his worthless life he'd sold something that was increasing in value. So what did he do? Rushed out here to offer you twice as much as you'd paid, quite certain you'd jump at the chance of a hundred per cent profit and never have the nous to stand back and wonder why a man like him should willingly let you make money. You were so blind greedy, you threw a million dollars down the bloody drain.'

He was so angrily humiliated that he answered back. 'And were you so very clever? What did you call me when I suggested you bought some of the shares? So naïve I thought Carey Street was a good address? The shares were worthless and always would be? So how much did you throw down the bloody drain? You could have bought a million shares and they'd be worth fifty million dollars now. So you've lost fifty million compared to my million. So who's the bigger fool?'

'How . . . how can you be so cruel and vicious?'

He was immediately contrite. 'I'm terribly sorry, Muriel, old girl. I was upset and didn't realize what I was saying . . .'

Only a complete idiot, thought Alvarez, would have apologized after forcing her on the defensive.

'If I had bought them,' she said sharply, determined to salvage her pride, 'I'd have known a damn sight better than to sell them back to him before I'd checked out why he wanted to buy.'

'I . . . I suppose you would.' Wheeldon stared down at his glass.

Alvarez said: 'Señor, when did you next meet Señor Taylor?'

'It was about three weeks ago.'

'Why did he come and see you this time? Was it still in connection with the Yabra Consolidated shares?'

'I don't remember.' He went over to the cocktail cabinet and poured himself a third pink gin.

She said: 'You must remember.' Her tone was sharp and clearly his earlier remarks had really hurt and now she was determined to gain revenge for his presumption. 'So if you don't want to talk about it, it must be embarrassing. I wonder what Steven said on his last visit that could so disturb you?' She paused, as if thinking. 'It surely can't be . . .?'

He looked appealingly at her.

'You know, Steven was always ridiculously proud of his ability to talk people into behaving like fools and the greater the challenge, the prouder he felt . . . Which means, of

course, that originally he couldn't gain much satisfaction
out of conning you.'

'Muriel, old girl . . .'

'I think he returned because he knew that by then you
would have discovered how he'd conned you out of a fortune
and you'd be sick with anger. Now, to sell more shares to
someone in that state would really be a challenge. Right?'

'I was only trying . . .'

'Your motto—always trying? What went on in your mind?
Did you manage to see yourself as a financier, making
and destroying financial empires with a brief nod of the
head?'

'Why won't you understand?'

'But I do, perfectly. I understand you just as thoroughly
as I understood my late, but unlamented, husband.'

'Señor,' said Alvarez, 'did you buy some more shares
from him?'

He looked at Alvarez with astonishment, as if he had
forgotten the detective was also present.

'Well, did you?' she said mockingly.

'He . . . he said it was a red-hot tip which he was telling
me about because in the circumstances he wanted to help
me. Don't you see how I . . .'

'Help? What genius, to use that word after he'd swindled
you out of a million dollars! But I don't suppose that even
now you've appreciated the full irony of it . . . How much
did he take you for this time?'

'I invested five hundred pounds.'

'Invested. How words change their meanings . . . And
you handed it over without a whimper; the sacrificial lamb,
running to its slaughter. He must have laughed himself
nearly sick.'

Alvarez knew pity, but also contempt, for Wheeldon; no
man should allow himself to be the butt of such vicious
contempt at the hands of a woman, however much he loved
her. He stood.

She looked up. 'Are you leaving? You're probably right. It looks as if the entertainment's over for the day.'

CHAPTER 17

Cala del Día—which in this context could loosely be translated as 'beach for the daytime—' was now the name given to a large area which included the urbanización and the complex of shops, cafés, and restaurants which served it, but originally it had pertained only to a very narrow strip of land which ran along the edge of a cliff. The name adumbrated Mallorquin humour; there was no beach, since the cliff plunged into the sea, and at night time, lacking any form of guard, it had been all too easy for a walker to tumble over the edge, especially on a fiesta.

Alvarez reached the foot of the urbanización and began the steep, zigzagging drive upwards. It was odd, he mused, how much the foreigners were prepared to pay for a view. To build on a slope cost up to fifty per cent more than on the level, especially if one demanded a large patio with pool. Yet all over the island there were developments along the lower slopes of hills and mountains. He modified his thoughts. He should be applauding his countrymen's business acumen rather than wondering at the gullibility of the foreigners. After all, such rocky slopes were otherwise valueless.

The road ended at Casa Resta, which stood on a fold of the mountain and therefore had views both to the east and the south; because of the steepness of the slope at this point, the outside of the foundations had had to be built up several metres. It was a large house, with a typically formless jumble of different roof levels; not much artistic talent would have been needed to make it far more visually appealing.

He rang the front-door bell. Rosa opened the door and

told him that the señor was down in the village, but would almost certainly be coming back soon—did he want to wait? She took him through the house to the patio. 'Feel like some coffee?'

'Mallorquin style?'

'What d'you think?'

As she went inside, he walked to the edge of the patio, just beyond the end of the swimming pool. At Ca'n Grande, one had the illusion of floating above the sea, here, the many houses in the urbanización below precluded any such fanciful thoughts; Ca'n Grande said there could be beauty in wealth, Casa Resta, only vulgarity.

Rosa returned to the patio with a tray on which were two cups of coffee, milk, sugar, and one balloon glass well filled with brandy. She set everything out on the patio table, sat. 'You can always hear him coming back.'

'He's the kind of man who wouldn't like to find you here?'

'Sometimes he'd laugh, sometimes he'd shout his head off. You just can't tell where you are with him. But he's a foreigner, so what d'you expect? Have anything to do with them?'

'Too much. I live in Llueso and sometimes I think half the population's foreign.'

'You're from Llueso? Then maybe you know my cousin from Playa Nueva?' She said that her cousin was a very cunning man who had made a fortune building houses on what had been a swamp. Almost all the houses were damp and the buyers were forever complaining. Wasn't it incredible that anyone could be so stupid as not to know that a house built on a swamp was going to be damp?

Alvarez returned the conversation to Reading-Smith. What kind of a man was he? A strange man. One minute he'd be friendly, the next he'd kick up hell. And if something refused to work, like the washing-machine or the toaster . . . She wondered if it was when he feared he was being made a fool of. But to think that of a machine! . . . There was, of course, something else which raised his temper. When he was getting fed up with whichever woman was living in the house. If he started shouting that the house was filthy and the housekeeping bills ridiculous, she knew that the current woman was on the way out. She often thought about the women. Had they no shame? Just because the señor was rich beyond the dreams of ordinary people, was that a reason for any woman to sell herself? But then, they were always foreigners. Mostly English. But there had been that French-woman who'd walked around the house naked. Not naked in a bathing costume; naked naked . . .

They heard the growl of an approaching high-powered car, its engine note rising and falling as it took the sharp bends.

'That's him.' She collected everything up.

'What's his woman situation at the moment?'

'A new one who'll be around for a while yet.' She picked up the tray. 'I remember our priest warning us that a special part of hell is reserved for fornicators. His place must have been booked a long time back.'

Soon after Rosa had returned into the house, Reading-Smith walked out on to the patio. There was no mistaking his essential toughness. It was in the cragginess of his face, the set of his mouth, the way he shook hands, and the tone of voice which made every statement a challenge.

'You're the police?'

'Yes, señor.'

'What d'you want?'

'To ask some questions concerning Señor Thompson.'

'Why?'

'I am investigating his death.'

'Does that mean it wasn't an accident?'

'Probably not.'

'I can't help you.'

'I think that perhaps you may be able to.'

Reading-Smith hesitated a moment, as if deliberating whether to throw Alvarez out, then said: 'It's like a bloody oven out here. We'll go inside.'

The sitting-room was air-conditioned and initially struck cold. Reading-Smith went over to an armchair, sat, hooked one leg over an arm. 'All right, let's hear how in the hell I'm supposed to be able to help.'

'Did you know that the señor's name was really Steven Taylor and his wife, Señora Muriel Taylor, lives in El Granero?'

'He was the husband of that stupid bitch? . . . Hang on. Her husband died years ago, back in England.'

'His death in England was faked.'

'Really?'

'Did you buy some shares from him?'

'If I want shares, I get my stockbroker to buy 'em, not a confidence trickster.'

'Why do you call him that?'

'If you've an ounce of intelligence, it stuck out a mile.'

'And you have many ounces of intelligence?'

'You've a quick tongue in your head, haven't you?'

'I don't know; but I doubt it is as quick as yours or the señor's. I've been told several times that his was very quick and very clever.'

'So?'

'I believe he persuaded you to buy four hundred thousand shares in an Australian mining company called Yabra Consolidated.'

'Believe what you bloody like.'

'You paid five cents when they were probably only worth two cents.'

'I'd have had to act like a bloody fool to do that.'

'Or to have listened too hard to his clever tongue . . . And when you'd realized what you'd done, your pride was very badly hurt. Which is why, when he returned and offered to buy back the shares at ten cents each, you immediately sold them without stopping to wonder at the reason for his making such an offer.'

Reading-Smith leaned forward and opened a silver cigarette case, helped himself to a cigarette, lit it.

'Later, you learned that the shares had increased greatly in value and your holding would have been worth two million Australian dollars.'

'So bloody what?' he shouted. He came to his feet and stood square to Alvarez.

The far door opened and a woman, wearing a string bikini, jet black hair falling down to her shoulders, stepped inside.

Reading-Smith swung round. 'What d'you bloody want?'

'I thought you called me.'

'I didn't. So get lost.'

'Bob, love, I really did think . . .'

He crossed the floor in five long strides, gripped her shoulders, swung her round, pushed her through the doorway, and slammed the door shut. He turned back. 'Have you finished?'

Clearly, the interruption—and brief physical action—had enabled him to regain his self-control and there was no longer a chance of needling him into angrily blurting out something he would later regret. Alvarez said: 'I've just one more question, señor.'

'You sound like my lawyer.' He returned to the chair.

'What did Señor Taylor want when he came here for the last time, roughly three weeks ago?'

He stubbed out the cigarette.

'Was it to sell you more shares?' Alvarez had been expecting a bitter denial, since otherwise this would have been to admit to having been made a fool a second time, but instead Reading-Smith said softly: 'That's right. He talked me into buying another five hundred quids' worth.'

Alvarez couldn't make head or tail of so ready an admission. He said goodbye and left.

As he settled behind the wheel of his car, he reflected that Steven Taylor's golden tongue and lack of any moral principles would surely have taken him right to the top in politics.

Alvarez braked the Seat to a stop on the hard shoulder, checked the dog-eared map of the island, and confirmed that although the straight line distance to Estruig was not very far, much of the journey was in the mountains and therefore would take at least an hour. From Estruig to Llueso, either by the shorter route over the mountains or the longer one returning to the plain, would take another hour which meant that if he visited Señora Swinnerton, he could not be expected to be home until well after eight . . . On the other hand, Comisario Borne was the kind of man who, if he discovered that one of his inspectors could have completed his work in one day, but hadn't . . . Regretfully, he decided to drive to Estruig.

Although he would not have liked to live up in the mountains—one had to be born among them to want to do that—he loved them, not least because they had not been despoiled in the name of tourism. The address he had was too indeterminate to locate Ca Na Muña unaided, but luckily he came across a man driving a mule cart, who'd been working in one of the fields in the small valley, and was directed along a dirt track which wound its way up an ever increasing slope until it came to a stop in front of a house. He climbed out of the car. What or who had originally driven a man to built his home here, where even a subsistence level of life called for endless toil? How many generations had it taken to build the terrace walls and carry up enough soil from the valley? And what kind of foreigner had chosen to live here, virtually cut off from all other human contact?

He climbed stone steps to the narrow level in front of the house, knocked on the door. There was a shout from further up the mountain and when he crossed to the side of the house and looked up he saw a woman who, laboriously and with an ungainly action, was descending more stone steps.

She reached the level. 'I'm sorry to keep you waiting like this,' she said breathlessly. She suddenly flinched.

'Is something wrong, señora?'

'It's just my leg. The beastly gout keeps plucking at me.'

He wondered why, if she suffered from gout, she had ever climbed up the terracing? He explained who he was.

'Do come on in and have a drink; it's such fun having someone to talk to! I'm afraid I've only wine, but at least there's plenty of that. And in case you're thinking that if I suffer from gout, I shouldn't drink, I'm happy to say that that myth was exploded some time ago!' She led the way to the front door. 'Mind how you go because the doorways are all so low; although you obviously don't have to be as careful as my husband did, but then he was tall and would walk around with his mind fixed on something else.'

The room they entered was both entrance hall and sitting-room. 'Which do you prefer, red or white?'

'I would like some red, please, señora.'

After she had gone through an arched doorway, he looked round the room. There was no missing the shabbiness. The covers of the two armchairs were frayed, the oblong carpet was faded and part threadbare, one of the two small wooden tables had a leg propped up by a wedge of newspaper, one curtain was missing, several floor tiles were cracked, and the walls and ceiling needed redecorating. Yet nowhere was there any sign of dirt or dust. It was the shabbiness of financial strain, not of sluttishness.

She returned with two glass tumblers and a litre bottle of wine. She filled the glasses and handed him one. 'David used to say that the vino corriente here was death to educated palates, but it didn't really matter because these days only expense-account businessmen and head waiters could afford to have one. I don't know enough about it to have an opinion, but his tastes certainly changed. After we'd been living here for a couple of years, he bought himself a special birthday treat of a very expensive bottle of Château Latour. He didn't enjoy it nearly as much as he'd expected and was quite happy to return to the usual Soldepeñas . . . But I'm quite certain you haven't come here to hear me go on and on rambling away, have you?'

'Señora, I am investigating the death of Señor Steven Taylor.'

'So you mentioned earlier, but I'm certain I've never met anyone with that name so I don't really see how I can help.'

'About three years ago he changed his name to Steven Thompson.'

'D'you mean the man who was killed in a car crash on the island? Good heavens! I was so sorry to read about that. So often the nicest people die before their time . . . He whom the gods favour dies young. So true and so sad . . . Now, what about Mr Thompson; or Mr Taylor, as you say his name really was?'

'Three years ago he was about to be arrested for fraud by the English police and so he faked his own death to escape —which was why he changed his name.'

'This island really does attract the most extraordinary people! David always said that the interesting foreigners who came to live here all had something to hide; being rather outspoken to me, he added that the uninteresting ones were far too boring ever to have done anything. I'd certainly never have guessed that Mr Taylor could have been like that because he was so friendly and amusing. Living on one's own, humour is one of the things one misses most. It's almost impossible to be funny with oneself.'

'Where did you meet him?'

'At a cocktail-party.' She chuckled as she looked down at the faded and patched print dress she was wearing. 'I know I hardly look like cocktail-party material at the moment, but I promise you that I can smarten up!'

'Did he sell you some shares?'

'How on earth did you know that?' She laughed again. 'Perhaps one ought to say that I persuaded him to sell them to me. You see, he'd stayed on after the party because he had a sudden attack of migraine and was hoping it would go before he needed to drive back and I'd stayed on because the Galbraiths had invited me to supper. He started talking to them about some shares which were absolutely bound to increase in value. He was very enthusiastic and obviously hoping the Galbraiths would buy some, but they're very rich and so they'll never do anything that isn't their idea in the first place. Anyway, I was thrilled because of the chance to make a little money and towards the end of the evening I buttonholed him and told him he must sell me some of the shares.'

'Forty thousand, I think?'

'Now tell me, how in the wide world did you discover that as well?'

'I had to search through his private papers and I found a note of the number of shares two or three people had bought.'

'And here was I beginning to think you must be clairvoyant!' She refilled her glass, passed the bottle across to him. 'You shouldn't have explained. Wasn't it Sherlock Holmes who said something to the effect that the brilliance of a deduction could never survive an explanation?'

'I'm afraid I don't know; I have never read any of the stories, only seen them on the television.'

'Not the same thing at all. The subtlety is lost. Especially, I imagine, in translation.'

'Señora, about two months later, you sold the shares back to him, didn't you?'

'That's correct. He turned up here and asked me if I'd like to sell them. He explained how the shares had risen in value and he wanted me to enjoy the profit. It was so kind of him.'

'And he bought them back at ten cents?'

'Indeed, and didn't charge any commission so that it was all profit. In two months, I more than doubled my money. It made me feel very guilty that originally, after I'd given him my cheque, I began to worry in case he wasn't quite honest. You see, I'd never met him before that night and if I'd lost all the money . . . It would have been quite terrible.'

He cleared his throat. 'Señora, I'm sorry, but I think you have to understand that when he sold you those shares they were probably really only worth two cents each.'

'He had to make a little money for all his trouble, didn't he? And he knew they were going to increase in value.'

'At the time he sold them to you, he did not expect them ever to increase in value.'

'Isn't that rather a nasty thing to say?'

'I'm afraid it's the truth. He was a swindler who was intent on swindling you.'

'How can you possibly say that when he more than doubled my money for me?'

'That only happened because unexpectedly the shares shot right up in value. And when he bought them back from you, he should have paid you five dollars a share, not ten cents.'

She was silent for a while, then she said quite firmly: 'I don't care, I shall remember him as someone who made me laugh and who helped me make some money.'

The contrast between her attitude towards events and those of Muriel Taylor, Wheeldon, and Reading-Smith, could hardly have been greater. He knew a sense of warm thankfulness that not everyone put money before all else. 'Señora, I wish there were more people who think like you,' he said impulsively.

'That's very kind of you. You really are the nicest possible detective!'

He felt slightly embarrassed and said hurriedly: 'I am afraid I have to ask you one more thing.'

'Don't worry. Talking with you is a real pleasure.'

'Did Señor Taylor come here about three weeks ago?'

'As a matter of fact, yes, he did.'

'That was to persuade you to buy some more shares?'

'It's funny you should say that because I told him I wanted to, but he wouldn't let me. No, he came to give me another thousand pounds.'

'He gave you money?'

'You sound surprised? I tell you, whatever his past is, he was a nice man. He said that when he'd sold the shares they'd done even better than he'd expected and he felt he owed me the extra.'

He now understood why she had repeatedly said that her money had been more than doubled. He thought he also understood the sequence of events. Taylor had originally met her at a cocktail-party given by very wealthy people and so he had imagined her to be, at the very least, reasonably well off; that she had not been expensively dressed would not have counted for much because a certain kind of rich woman was often eccentric in some matters. But when he had first visited her in her house he had immediately realized that far from being wealthy, she was poor. So he had later given her the money he had just swindled out of Wheeldon and Reading-Smith (the third act of swindling, by which he had proved to himself that he really was the best), enjoying to the full the role of Robin Hood . . .

A quarter of an hour and another glass of wine later, he said he must leave. She hoped he'd come again and he replied that he certainly would if he could think of an excuse that would fool his superior chief.

He was outside, about to go down the stone steps to his car, when she said: 'I wish you had come here a few years ago.'

'Why, señora?'

'Because then we were both alive and well and the whole of the garden was a mass of colour. David used to say that one of the few things created by man that was truly beautiful was the garden. He wrote a lovely poem about that.'

'There is still a lot of colour.'

She looked up, shading her eyes from the sun with her hand. 'But it's not like it used to be. And my gardener's finally left so now the weeds will grow unchecked and the only flowers which will survive will be those which don't need watering and don't mind being crowded . . . But I shouldn't really talk like that. David loved a cultivated garden, but he believed that a natural one, even with all its weeds, was still beautiful.' She tilted her head back as she looked even higher. 'Do you know why I shall remember Mr Taylor for the nice things he did, not the nasty?'

It was clearly a rhetorical question.

'Because the money he made me helped to make certain I can live here just a little longer.'

He finally said goodbye and left. As he drove away, he felt both uplifted and saddened; uplifted because she had proved that there were still those who were untouched by avarice, saddened because she had shown that old age was a time when one had to search too hard to find compensation for living.

CHAPTER 18

As Alvarez left his parked car and walked towards the nearer back door of Las Cinco Palmeras, something began to bother him. Only as he knocked on the door of the kitchen did he identify what that something was—the silence.

'Who is it?' Helen called out.

'Enrique Alvarez, señora.'

'Come on in.'

She was wearing damp, stained overalls over a T-shirt. 'You don't by any chance know anything about plumbing, do you?'

'I regret not.'

'I've been trying to make a tap work and can't. Soon, I shall assault it with the biggest hammer I can find.'

'But why are the builders not here? I saw Javier and he promised to start work just as soon as he could. I will go now and see him and tell him that if he doesn't come immediately . . .'

She brushed some hair away from her forehead. 'Don't waste your time.' Her tone was suddenly bitter.

'I can promise you . . .'

'He turned up and said he'd start the moment his bill was paid.'

'But I thought . . .'

'So did I. But Mike, the silly fool, never told me the truth because he was trying to protect me from the worry. Practically all the money Mike's father gave him for the repairs was paid out for the funeral.'

'Oh!' There was really nothing more he could find to say immediately. Then he struggled to reintroduce a note of optimism. 'Perhaps if he spoke to one of the other and smaller builders, he could persuade them to do the work now, but wait to be paid until you are open and making money?'

'Mike thought of that right away. He's seen every local firm and not one of them will do it. The trouble seems to be, quite a few foreigners haven't been paying their bills once their houses are finished because they've learned how slow the law moves and how difficult it is to recover a debt. One or two are even boasting about how clever they are in not paying—God, what I could do to them! . . . When you arrived, I was trying to see if I could do some of the work. I've discovered I can't . . . Anyway, that's enough of that.

What's brought you here this time—not more trouble, please.'

'I hope it won't be that,' he answered uncomfortably, 'but I have to speak to the señor.'

'He went off to see someone who might lend us the money in return for a stake in the restaurant. The trouble is, this person wants such a large stake. I suppose you can't really blame him because it's good business. But I'm always so stupid I hope people will help in the same way that I'd try to help them.'

He wished he had the money to offer and so drive away from her blue eyes the worry that filled them.

They heard the whine of the approaching Citroën van.

'Go and sit out in the front,' she said, making a determined attempt to lighten her mood, 'and I'll send Mike out with a drink.'

'There's no need for that.'

'We've plenty of alcohol, if nothing else.'

He went through the restaurant and sat at the nearest table, in the shade of a palm tree. A couple of minutes later Taylor, a glass in each hand, came out. 'What the hell is it this time?' His manner suggested that the meeting with the possible backer had not been successful.

'I have just returned from Corleon—did you know that that is where your father lived?'

'I told you last time, I'd no idea where he was.'

'With him lived a friend; a very beautiful young lady.'

'He always did have good taste.'

'The house and large yacht were bought in her name and so now are hers.'

'That ought to help dry a few of her tears.'

'But did you know that under his will, you are his sole beneficiary?'

'How the hell could I?'

'He must have discussed the matter with you.'

'Maybe he must, but he bloody didn't.'

'Nevertheless, as his only child, you must have expected this?'

'I expected nothing.'

'Where are his assets?'

'How would I know?'

'You father must have told someone so that they could be distributed according to his will after his death.'

'Like as not, he didn't have any to worry about.'

'Why do you say that? A man doesn't usually spend all his money and so leave himself without any reserves.'

'My old man didn't know about "usually". He subscribed to Barnum's philosophy—there's a sucker born every minute. So when he needed money, he went out and found a sucker.'

'He gave you the money to buy this restaurant and to meet the cost of the original repairs?'

'Where's the problem? Obviously, he'd just found a sucker.'

'In fact, he'd found at least three. He sold them Australian mining shares at five cents when they were probably only worth two.'

'That's my father.'

'He bought them back at ten cents because by then they stood at around five dollars. He made about three million dollars.'

Taylor stared at Alvarez for several seconds, then laughed. 'So the old bastard really did find El Dorado!'

'Where do you think all that money is?'

'The answer remains, I've no idea.'

'Are you certain of that?'

'What are you trying to get at?' Taylor's expression sharpened. 'Last time you were here, you were talking about the possibility my father was poisoned.'

'That is correct.'

'Was he?'

'The results of the post mortem aren't yet through.'

'But you're behaving as if they were. You're bloody

wondering if I murdered him for the three million dollars, aren't you?'

'I have to investigate that possibility.'

'It hasn't occurred to your sweeping intelligence that if I had, I wouldn't now be tearing out my hair trying to find the money to pay the builders?'

'Perhaps the safest way of concealing new wealth would be to give the appearance of remaining hard up.'

'You've a mind like a bloody sewer. He was my father.'

'Sadly, sons murder fathers. And as you have told me, the relationship between the two of you was less than close.'

They heard the sounds of Helen's coming out of the restaurant and turned to watch her approach. 'I wondered if you were ready for another drink?'

Taylor said bitterly: 'Remember telling me what a wonderful man the Inspector was: so kind and thoughtful and not at all like a policeman?'

'What on earth's the matter?'

'Your wonderfully kind and thoughtful inspector has just accused me of murdering my own father.'

'No, señor, I did not say that,' objected Alvarez quietly. 'I said that I have to investigate the possibility that you did; if indeed he was murdered. That means establishing whether you had a motive—and you had. But in this, you are not alone. There are four other people who also had one.'

'Who?'

'The three whom he tricked out of a great deal of money and Señorita Benbury, who may well know where the fortune is held and is determined to get hold of it for herself.'

CHAPTER 19

Alvarez was pouring himself a second brandy when the telephone rang. Juan said he'd answer it and ran out of the dining-room into the front room. Dolores said from the kitchen doorway: 'When you've finished drinking, the meal's ready.'

'Give it a quarter of an hour,' replied Jaime.

'You are not going to eat?'

'Of course I am. What . . .'

'Then your drinking's finished.' She returned into the kitchen.

'Women!' he muttered, as he looked at his empty glass and the bottle. 'I've a good mind to . . .' He did not specify what. It wasn't that he was afraid of incurring Dolores's wrath—no Mallorquin husband could ever be so weak—but experience had taught him that her standards of cooking varied according to her humour and he greatly enjoyed his food.

Juan returned. 'The call's for you, Uncle.'

'Who is it?' asked Alvarez.

'Someone who talks very fast.'

Off-hand, he couldn't think of anyone who spoke particularly quickly.

He carried his glass through to the front room, drank just before he said: 'Yes?'

'This is Borne speaking.'

'Who is it?'

'I said, this is Comisario Borne.'

'I'm sorry, Comisario. It's just that my nephew—who isn't really my nephew—said that the caller spoke very fast, not that it was you, and I was wondering who it could be and then you said Borne and I have a friend who's name is rather like that, but he doesn't live in Palma and you don't sound like him and I was a bit confused.'

'Clearly. I am ringing to inform you that a telex has just arrived from England. It reads: Re Steven Taylor stop Private investigator identified as Raymond Barton stop Retained on eighteenth April to investigate Steven Thompson who was described as fraudulently selling shares in Mallorca stop Through unidentified police contacts Barton finally identified Thompson as Steven Taylor stop Transmitted to client full details of Taylor's criminal record and supposed death stop Client's name Reading-Smith address Casa Resta Cala del Día stop Hope it's stair-rodding with you stop Ian Wallace . . . Do you understand the meaning of that last sentence?'

'I think, señor, that Detective-Sergeant Wallace is hoping that it's raining here because the weather in England is so bad.'

'Were I his senior officer, I would point out that that is not a subject for an official message. Does the information assist you?'

'To be frank, señor, I'm not quite certain. I'll have to sit back and think about it.'

'Then will you please do that. Have you received a report on the post mortem?'

'Not yet.'

'Has it occurred to you to point out to the Institute that the matter is of very considerable urgency?'

'Yes. But I don't think that that had much effect.'

'You do realize, do you, that it is essential before any real progress can be made in this case to know for certain whether or not we are dealing with a murder?'

'Yes, señor.'

'Superior Chief Salas asked me this afternoon whether I thought you had yet grasped that fact. I had to reply that it was very difficult, if not impossible, to give a definite opinion.'

'Señor, I have been doing my best.'

'Possibly. Superior Chief Salas further remarked that most regretfully you always seem concerned more with irrelevancies than those matters which are pertinent.'

'I'm afraid he doesn't seem to understand that I like to get to know as much about the background of all the people in a case as possible.'

'It is very seldom an advantage to undertake a disorganized approach. Concentrate, Inspector; concentrate on the points which matter and ignore those which do not.'

'Yes, señor.'

Borne said a distant good night, rang off. Alvarez sighed as he replaced the receiver. Life was so simple for superiors. They demanded information and issued orders and then did not have to concern themselves about the means . . .

'Enrique, are you coming?' Dolores called out. 'It's getting cold.'

He drained the glass. He thought that he now understood why Reading-Smith had so readily admitted that he'd been conned into buying a second load of shares, when his character suggested his reaction would have been one of angry denial.

Alvarez rang the Institute of Forensic Pathology at midday and spoke to Professor Fortunato's secretary.

'As a matter of fact, Inspector, I was just about to get in touch with you to tell you that the post mortem has been completed and it is established—not that, of course, there was ever any real doubt—that actual death was due to injuries received in the crash. There are no obvious signs of poisoning and further and more detailed tests are to be carried out.'

Alvarez thanked the secretary, then rang the forensic laboratory.

'In the sample listed "Corleon", the content of all the capsules was correct; in the sample listed "deceased", the content of two capsules was the poison colchicine.'

'What exactly is that?'

'It's a vegetable poison which comes from the Meadow Saffron and is a cytotoxin, or cell poison. Each of the capsules contained approximately eight milligrammes of the poison, together with neutral binders, which is generally held to be a less than fatal dose for an adult in good health —not that one can ever be dogmatic on that score.'

'Would it be easy to get hold of the stuff?'

'Nothing easier, if you live somewhere where the plant grows wild. I was on holiday once and saw a field almost carpeted with them. I can remember looking at the colourful picture and wondering just how many people that one field could kill . . . Virtually every part of the plant contains colchicine, although the flowers, seeds, and corms contain the greatest concentration.'

'How soon would it start to work after swallowing?'

'Very difficult to say because that depends on so many variables—how long since the last meal, what did that consist of, how susceptible is the victim . . . But say between three and six hours after ingestion, remembering that any figure can be wrong.'

'What are the symptoms?'

'They're very similar to those of arsenical poisoning, which is why it's sometimes called vegetable arsenic. One's throat and mouth begin to burn and there's tremendous thirst, but when one goes to drink there's considerable trouble in swallowing. Pretty soon, one's suffering violent nausea and vomiting. These symptoms can last as long as twenty-four hours before the really serious ones start— agonizing colics, paralysis of the central nervous system, growing difficulty in breathing. It can take up to another twenty-four hours to die. So if you've someone you really dislike, feed him some!'

'I just hope there's no Meadow Saffron growing round our way.'

The assistant laughed. 'I can name another dozen plants just as deadly, or even more so. And actually, it's got its good side as well as its bad. For quite a time now, tests have been carried out using therapeutic doses in some cases of arthritis and I believe there have been some very encouraging results.'

'I'll stick to aspirins.'

'Watch it. Take too many of them and you're in trouble.'

Alvarez rang off. At last they were certain. Someone had tried to murder Steven Taylor and although he had not died from the poison, his death was directly attributable to it.

CHAPTER 20

Alvarez left his car, walked up to the front door of Casa Resta, and knocked. Rosa opened the door. 'You again!'

'Is the señor in?'

'He and his woman are out for the day on the boat; I had to prepare the picnic lunch for them.'

'Damn!'

'But you might just catch him if you hurry because they're not long gone and they were buying some rolls on the way.'

'What's the name of his boat?'

'It's something like . . .' She stopped and thought, frowning heavily. 'I can't remember, except it's an English name. But you can't mistake which one it is because it's almost at the end of the breakwater and it's the biggest there.'

'Sail or motor?'

'Motor, I suppose. I mean, it must be, seeing it's not got a real mast.'

He returned to his car and drove down to the village and the port. There was no bay to offer natural protection from heavy seas and winds and so two curving breakwaters had been built; these were wide and they provided moorings on their inboard sides. Rosa had not said whether the boat was tied up to the port or starboard arm, but cars could only drive along the starboard one and this was clearly where the larger boats berthed. Alvarez parked two-thirds of the way along, then walked past several yachts and motor-cruisers of increasing size, a surprising number of which flew the British flag, suggesting to him that despite all their hypocritical claims, the British were no less astute at avoiding their tax claims than the Continentals.

He approached the largest boat present and the fact that this was Reading-Smith's was confirmed when a bikini-clad figure came out of the accommodation and walked for'd. If that were really possible, Vera's costume was even skimpier than the one she had been wearing when he had seen her up at the house.

There was a small gangplank, rigged with a single set of ropes, and because the stern of the boat rode high it tilted upwards at a steep angle. He stepped on to it, gripped the top rope very tightly with his left hand, and tried not to think about the gap that was opening up either side of his feet. It was absolutely ridiculous, but even now his altophobia was flooding his mind with fear.

He reached the head of the gangplank and thankfully stepped on to the deck to realize that Reading-Smith was now standing immediately outside the accommodation and had obviously been watching his ascent. Vera, by his side, was giggling.

'I'll give you a piece of free advice,' Reading-Smith said boisterously. 'Don't think of serving before the mast.'

He had never done so.

'What's it this time? And you'd better be bloody quick because we're sailing in five minutes.'

'I have some more questions.'

'If you got paid by the dozen, you'd be rich. Questions about what?'

'Señor Taylor's death.'

'I suppose you want a drink? After your dangerous climb, I'd say it was a bloody necessity!' He turned and went into the accommodation, followed by Vera.

The saloon was twenty feet long and almost the width of the boat. Aft, there were several easy chairs and two bulkhead settees, amidships a table and dining chairs, and for'd a small bar, complete with bar stools. Reading-Smith went behind the bar and opened a bottle of champagne; Vera settled on one of the aluminium-legged stools.

'All right, what are the questions?' Reading-Smith filled a tulip-shaped glass and handed it to Vera.

'First of all, señor, I must tell you that now we know for certain that Señor Taylor was poisoned before the crash. The poison was administered by substituting it for the contents of at least three capsules he was in the habit of taking to counter a threatened migraine. The amount of poison he swallowed was not sufficient to make him so ill he could no longer drive and, despite being very sick, he would not let his companion take the wheel. As a result, and due to a fresh attack of nausea, he misjudged his driving and the car crashed and he was killed. Because the sequence of events stems directly from the giving of the poison, his death was murder.'

As Reading-Smith passed Alvarez a glass, he said: 'All very interesting, but what's it to do with me?'

'It's now my duty to discover whether it was you who filled the capsules with poison.'

'Why the hell should I have done that?'

'You see yourself as a clever and sharp businessman, don't you?'

'Do I?'

'But Señor Taylor proved that you are neither.'

'Any more compliments?'

'Do be careful,' murmured Vera.

He swung round. 'Why don't you just shut up?'

'But you can't talk like that to a policeman . . .'

'On my own boat, I'll talk how I bloody well like.'

'You must have wanted to murder Señor Taylor,' said Alvarez, 'when he made a fool of you for the third time?'

'That's a bloody lie.'

'Do you remember telling me that you'd never buy shares from anyone other than your stockbroker? Yet you bought a large number of shares from him.'

'You don't understand.'

'That he had a golden tongue? Oh, yes, señor, I have understood that from the beginning. But you didn't—and that surprises me. After all, I am a simple islander while you are a clever and successful businessman and, I'd have thought, far too clever to be caught.' Alvarez's tone changed as he set out to goad Reading-Smith. 'But then I remind myself that the smarter a man believes himself, the easier it is to catch him. Which is why Señor Taylor was able to persuade you to sell him back the shares at a fiftieth of their true value. He could judge exactly how best to persuade you. You'd be so eager to cover up your own stupidity, especially from yourself, that you'd rush to have him buy them back because for you, to be clever is to make money and he was offering you the chance to make some; it would only be later that you'd stop to wonder why he was offering you such a chance. And when you worked out the answer, you must have been very, very angry.'

Reading-Smith drained his glass, refilled it.

'Bob . . .' Vera began.

'Clear out.'

She was frightened by the expression on his face. She slid off the stool and hurried out of the saloon by way of the for'd starboard door.

Alvarez said: 'Perhaps the most incredible fact is that you let him make a fool of you a third time!'

'Like bloody hell I did.'

'Didn't you? Despite everything, he was still able to persuade you to buy more shares from him.'

'You think I bought 'em because he was still taking me for a sucker?'

'Naturally.'

'You're so bloody wrong . . .' He stopped.

'Yes?'

He struggled to contain his anger.

'Señor, were you going to say that you let him sell you more shares not because you were still a fool, but because then he was in your house long enough for you to substitute poison for the contents of some of the capsules in the medicine bottle?'

'No.'

'You had the motive for his murder. Every time you thought about how he'd been laughing at you, you must have hated him a bit more. Someone of your character would have to get his own back.'

'But not by murdering him,' Reading-Smith shouted.

'To a naturally violent person, that's the obvious solution.'

'I . . .'

'Yes?'

He angrily shook his head.

'What alerted you to the fact that he might have a criminal record? His professionalism? You were convinced that only a true professional could have swindled you so easily?'

'What's it matter?'

'It should matter to you. That is, if you don't wish to be arrested for murder.'

'I didn't poison him.'

'Prove it.'

'How the hell can I prove a bloody negative?'

'By telling me the truth.'

Because the admission would portray himself in so nasty a light, Reading-Smith tried desperately to find a way out of making it, but even through his anger it became obvious that it was his only way of escaping arrest.

He spoke quickly, his voice thick. Yes, he'd determined to get his own back on the smart bastard—but not by committing murder. He'd hired a private detective in England to find out about Steven Thompson, a professional swindler who'd worked a racket with shares. Eventually, the detective had discovered that Thompson's real name was Taylor and that he'd had one conviction and was facing a second one when he'd conveniently 'died' in a car crash.

This had given Reading-Smith the handle he'd been seeking. There was now an extradition agreement between Spain and Britain. Unfortunately, it was not retrospective because Spanish law did not permit this and so there could be no extradition for a crime committed before the passing of the act, but the Spaniards had a genius for attaining a desired result by devious means if the direct one proved impossible; they'd introduced a further law which gave the authorities the right to expel any foreigner whose habits were likely to bring the country into disrepute. Under this law, Taylor could be expelled; once expelled, he'd either have to return to the UK and face arrest or move to another country— where the extradition laws would probably catch him. So obviously what was necessary was to provoke Taylor into committing an act which would render him liable to arrest, and extradition (now the act was in force) or to expulsion. It had been quite a problem . . . Until, incredibly, blinded by his own pride, he'd turned up again, offering to sell more shares. The next move became obvious. Buy the shares, prove they were worthless and Taylor must have known they were, introduce the evidence which showed that Taylor was a professional swindler, and the authorities wouldn't, at the very least, hesitate to expel him. Then warn the British police to keep their eyes open . . .

'And you'd have had the satisfaction of knowing he was spending the next few years in jail,' said Alvarez contemptuously.

Alvarez entered the tall, ancient building that was the town hall in Mentaña and spoke to a clerk who referred him to a second man who referred him to a third. The last, having no one else to whom he could reasonably send Alvarez, reluctantly agreed to consult the property books.

'Señor the Honourable Archibald Wheeldon . . .' He stumbled over the pronunciations. '. . . lives in Calle General Castillo Martínez, fifteen.'

'Is that here, in Mentaña?'

He replied with indignation that everyone knew that Calle General Castillo Martínez was in Mentaña; had not the General been born only two streets away from where they now were? And hadn't the Caudillo himself said that if only he'd had two more generals with the fire and dash of Castillo, he'd have won the Civil War within six months . . .

Alvarez left. The way was not steep, nevertheless by the time he reached the famous road he was breathing very heavily and sweating profusely. He remembered his recent, and second, promise to cut back on eating, drinking, and smoking, and assured himself that tomorrow he really would honour that promise.

No. 15, one in a long line of terrace houses, of different roof levels, which directly fronted the narrow road, was in obvious need of decoration and at least some light repairs; the paint on the shutters was peeling off and patches of rendering had fallen. He knocked on the front door, since a foreigner lived there, and waited. After a time, the door was opened. 'Good morning,' said Wheeldon. Then he hastily corrected his Spanish to, 'Good afternoon.'

'Good afternoon, señor,' replied Alvarez in English. 'May I have a word with you?'

Wheeldon looked perplexed until he identified his caller and then his manner became nervous. 'Aren't you the detective chappie who was at Muriel's . . . that is, at Señora Taylor's?'

'That's right.'

'Nice to see you again,' he said with patent insincerity.

They went through one room, used as a hall, into a second one which was filled with large, heavy, and rather uncomfortable local furniture.

'What can I get you? A cup of coffee? Or is it not too early for a drink?'

'On this island, señor, we have a saying—it can never be too early for a drink, only too late.'

'That's rather good. I must try and remember it. So what would you like?'

After he'd served the drinks, Wheeldon sat, then said: 'Are you busy? I don't suppose there's much crime here, of course . . .'

'These days there is, sadly, a growing amount.'

'Bit difficult to understand that. I mean, everyone's so sleepy . . . Oh! Please don't misunderstand me. Much of the charm is . . .' Again, he tailed off into silence, finally aware of the fact that it would be better if he did not try to explain.

'I have received the results of the post mortem on Señor Taylor.'

'Really? Nasty thought. I mean, knowing what they do to the body . . . I was sorry he died in that crash. Cheerful kind of a chap with a fund of amusing stories. Of course, he did have a bit of a history which makes him . . . Not that I knew all about that at the time.'

'He was poisoned.'

'My God!'

'He crashed as a direct result of the poisoning, so now I am investigating a case of murder.'

'I suppose you must be.'

'I need to know who had a motive for the murder.'

'Yes, I can see that, but why come here? I mean, I hardly knew the man.'

'You bought shares from him and then sold them back to him.'

'Yes, but . . . Look, I made money doing that.'

'Not nearly as much as you should have done.'

Wheeldon gesticulated with his hands, as if trying to suggest that that was of small account.

'He should have paid you a million Australian dollars, shouldn't he?

'Yes, but . . .'

'That offers a very strong motive.'

'For killing him? Can't you understand, I couldn't ever do such a thing.'

'Why not?'

'Why not? But you've got to know, why not.'

'Have I?'

Miserably, he tried to explain, leaving out any personal details because a gentleman did not discuss such matters—nevertheless, it was easy to fill in the omissions. He was in love with Muriel. She could be difficult, she could embarrass, but he loved her. And as far as he was concerned, her money was of no account because a gentleman did not marry for money and remain a gentleman. Unfortunately, she had not been born to money—which was not to suggest for one second that she had married the first time because of it—and so she saw it as a status symbol and a measure of . . . well, worth as a person. And unfortunately, like others in her position, she suspected people of being friendly because of her money, not in spite of it. Her second marriage hadn't helped. With his golden tongue, Steven Taylor had silenced her suspicions and reservations long enough to persuade her to marry him, but afterwards, when things had gone wrong, all her prejudices had been reinforced. So when he, Wheeldon, had fallen in love with her, she had . . . Well, even though they were good friends, she would not marry him because he didn't have much money. Unfortunately, he was old-fashioned enough to want to be married. Taylor had turned up—of course, at the time he'd had no idea that Taylor was her 'dead' husband—and had talked about shares that were bound to rise in value and it had all sounded so attractive that he'd done something he'd never done before and that was to risk a part of his very limited capital because he'd believed that if only he could make some money, Muriel would then be able to realize that he loved her for herself. When Taylor had offered him twice what he'd paid, he'd naturally jumped at the chance of a hundred per cent profit. A few more deals like that . . . He'd read in a paper about the spectacular rise of the shares and had learned that he'd parted with the fortune he was so desperate to obtain . . .

'So what were your feelings towards Señor Taylor?'

'I . . . Well, I . . .'

'You must have hated him?'

'I suppose so.'

'Sufficiently to wish him dead?'

'Of course not.'

'Why not? He'd deprived you of what you'd most wanted.'

'My God, you can't think like that! I couldn't ever get so worked-up as a Mallorquin would . . .' He stopped.

'That is very true. An islander has a violent argument and before he thinks what he's doing, he pulls out a knife and uses it. But poisoning is not a hot-blooded act, it is a cold-blooded one.'

'That's not what I'm trying to say. I'd never think of murder just because I'd been swindled.'

'Not even the third time?'

'What d'you mean, the third time?'

'Señor Taylor sold you more shares.'

'Yes, but they . . . they may rise in value just as Yabra Consolidated did.'

'Have you checked that they are worth at least as much as you paid for them?'

Wheeldon shook his head.

'Why not?'

'I . . . Well, the truth is, if they turn out to be worth a lot less, it'll make me look such a fool.'

'I'd prefer to say, too trusting.'

'You must believe me.'

Alvarez stood. 'I do,' he said sadly.

CHAPTER 21

Alvarez walked into the chemist shop and spoke to the husband, who had just finished serving a customer. The husband led the way into the stock room.

'I want to find out something. I gather colchicine is a pretty potent poison?'

'That's right.'

'But even so, it's used therapeutically?'

'Lots of poisons are; maybe they all could be if we knew enough about 'em—natural, not manmade poisons, that is. I've heard it claimed that that's one more proof that the universe is totally symmetrical; there's always a plus to balance a minus. Frankly, that sort of stuff leaves me cold, but it is a hard fact that a poison like colchicine can cure as well as kill.'

'What's it used for medically?'

'As far as I know, just the treatment of arthritis. I read not so long ago that its use is being extended and there have been promising results in cases of rheumatoid arthritis.'

'Extended from what?'

'From its traditional field, which is gout.'

Friday morning brought the first clouds for days, but as the sun rose higher these were slowly burned away and by eleven the sky was once again clear and the sun shone with burning brilliance. Alvarez parked in front of the stone stairs which led up to Ca Na Muña, turned off the engine, stepped out. One by one, the cicadas, which had been disturbed by his arrival, resumed their shrilling; overhead, but not immediately locatable, came the sharp cry, twice repeated, of a raptor; a branch of a tree, moving in the very light breeze, scraped against something with a soft, rhythmic sound; the air was heady with the scent of wild thyme.

Valerie came out of the house, her movements slightly easier than when he had last seen her, and she met him at the head of the steps. 'Hullo again. I hope you've come for a long chat?'

'Señora, I fear that I have to ask you more questions.'

'Why be sorry? I told you last time, I'm delighted to have someone to talk to. Now, come on in and we'll have a glass of wine.'

'Perhaps we should have the questions first.'

'Good heavens, no! You'll be able to ask much nicer ones and I'll be able to answer them much more wisely if we have a drink beforehand.'

He followed her into the coolness of the house. A newspaper was on the floor by the side of one of the chairs and she bent down and picked this up. 'I went into the village yesterday and met some friends and they gave me this copy of the *Daily Telegraph*. I rather wish they hadn't. Britain's become a dreadful place because of all the crime.'

'There's crime on this island. Señor Taylor was poisoned.'

'Was he? Oh dear! What a horrid way to die.'

'He didn't die from poisoning, but because of it; that's what caused him to crash.'

'I suppose there is a difference?'

'Yes, although it remains a murder.'

'I know it's wanting to bury my head in the sand, but can't we talk about something nicer?'

'I'm afraid not. That's what I have come to discuss.'

'Oh dear! . . . Anyway, let me get the drinks first. Would you still prefer red wine?'

She went out into the kitchen, returned with two tumblers of wine, one of which she handed to him. 'This is a different wine which I bought yesterday in the village; the woman in the shop told me it was much nicer than the one I usually have.' She smiled. 'Perhaps she couldn't sell it to anyone else, so decided to unload it on a fool foreigner.'

'Señora, I have just been to the town hall in Estruig. I asked them for the date on which Señor Swinnerton died. They could find no record of the señor's death. I then asked them to check burials. There was no record of the señor's burial. Yet I distinctly remember your telling me that he died in this house. In such a case, it was necessary to notify the town hall in Estruig and for the burial to take place in Estruig cemetery.'

There was a silence.

'Why did you not notify the authorities of the señor's death?'

'What does it matter now?'

'Where is he buried?'

She gave no answer.

'Last time I was here, you walked down from the terraces above and you were moving with difficulty because of pain from gout. Crippled to such an extent, you would surely only have climbed up if there were some very important reason to do so.' He waited, but she remained silent. 'Señora, is your husband buried up on one of the terraces?'

She seemed to shiver; seen in profile, her heavy face held an expression of sad resignation. She said in a low, distant voice, 'He knew he was dying, but thought I didn't. For as long as he could he pretended that he was feeling better and I pretended that I believed him . . .

'Then he became too weak to move. He lay on the settee in the other room because the window's so low and he could look out at the mountains he loved so much. Towards the end, he wasn't fully conscious and quite often he asked why it was so hot. I tried to explain that we weren't in Wales, but he couldn't understand. Once or twice, he thought I was his mother . . .

'On the last day his mind suddenly cleared and he knew that I knew. He told me that our marriage had always been so happy that he'd dreaded the bill—he was so certain that happiness always had to be paid for. He talked about the garden and how he hoped there really was a life after death so that he could keep the picture of the garden together with the picture of me. He told me how he wished he could be buried amid the garden and not in a cemetery, hemmed in by walls and frowned on by tombs which had been built to impress. He was talking about the beauty all around here only seconds before he died . . .

'I knew that I had to give him what he had most wanted.' Tears were trickling down her furrowed cheeks, but her voice held steady. 'I buried him on one of the terraces, near the twisted olive tree he called the Laocöon, I don't care how wrong that was.'

'Señora, nothing that so strong a love does can be truly wrong.'

'Do you . . . Do you really believe that?'

'Yes.'

'Thank God . . . It's all become so difficult since David died. You see, he never understood how to manage the money we had and so there wasn't much left and no matter how hard I tried, because everything had become so expensive I had to keep using a little of the capital. One day I discovered that very soon I wouldn't be able to afford to live here any longer. That would mean leaving David and I couldn't bear to think of doing that . . .

'I went to the cocktail-party where I met Mr Thompson and he talked about how easy it was to make money if you knew what you were doing . . . I thought that if I could make some money, perhaps I could stay here until I died and then I would have kept faith with David. So I asked Mr Thompson to sell me some shares. And the next time I saw him, he said that they had gone up until they were worth twice as much and he strongly advised me to sell and take the profit before they went down again, as he expected them to do. The extra money meant that I could stay here a little longer and look after David. I told Mr Thompson how grateful I was and he said that it was helping people like me which made his life so worthwhile.

'I was in Estruig one day and in a newspaper I read about the shares. They were worth fifty times what he'd paid me. If he'd given me the proper price, I would have had enough money not only to be certain I could go on living here until I died, but also to employ a gardener again so that David was surrounded by his favourite flowers . . .

'Mr Thompson came to the house. I begged him to give me the extra money and explained why I needed it. He said . . .'

'What did he say, señora?'

'That a promise to someone who was dead was meaningless.'

'A man like him could never understand.'

'He gave me another thousand pounds . . . He made it seem he was doing me a favour instead of having cheated me. I couldn't bear it . . . I kept thinking of David . . .'

'So you poisoned him?'

She opened her mouth to speak, said nothing.

He thought he understood her sequence of emotions. She was a woman of peace and love and was shocked and horrified by what she'd done. She believed in forgiveness and redemption, but only after expiation. So having poisoned Taylor, she wanted to expiate her sin, which meant she should now confess and suffer the penalties the law decreed. But imprisonment would mean deserting David . . .

He had to be certain of the details. 'You suffer from gout and one treatment is to take therapeutic doses of colchicine. You knew that this was a poison and it was dangerous to take more than the prescribed dose. You had learned that Steven Taylor suffered from migraine and had seen the capsules he always carried around with him, so you got hold of the bottle, extracted some of the capsules, emptied these and refilled them with as much of your ground-up pills as you could get into them. Sooner or later, he would swallow one of these poisoned pills and, you hoped, would die.'

'No,' she said fiercely.

He looked at her with pity. 'Where are the pills you take to alleviate your gout?'

'I don't have any.'

'If necessary, I will search this house.'

'All right, I do take some. But I didn't do as you've just said.'

'Will you get them for me, please.'

She stood, left. He heard her slowly climbing the stairs, which led out of the next room, then crossing overhead, her footsteps loud because the floor was bare concrete. When she returned, she handed him a bottle half-full of small round green pills.

'Do you have any more of these?'

'No.'

'Then I'll only take a few.'

'Aren't . . . aren't you arresting me?'

'Since you deny having substituted some of these pills for the contents of the capsules, I have to prove that that is what you did—at the moment, I have no such proof. Indeed, it's not even certain that these pills contain colchicine.'

'But you'll find the proof?'

'I'm afraid I probably will, señora.'

'And then you'll arrest me?'

Being a coward, he was glad that now it would be the superior chief and not he who would initiate the actual arrest.

CHAPTER 22

On Tuesday, a south wind brought the heat and the sand of the Sahara; everything in the open became covered in fine sand and the temperature rose above a hundred so that even the foreigners left their homes shuttered throughout the day. Villages appeared to be deserted.

At breakfast, Dolores had asked Alvarez to drive on from the port—when he'd finished his work there—to Playa Nueva to buy some cold smoked pork from the German shop and he remembered this as he passed the petrol station on his way back to Llueso. He swore, stopped the car on the hard shoulder, and looked at his watch. Nearly half twelve. If he now drove over to Playa Nueva he would not be home much before a quarter past one and for the past hour he'd been looking forward with ever increasing impatience to the first iced brandy. On the other hand, if he didn't get the pork, Dolores would not be best pleased . . .

He waited for two cars to pass, made a U-turn. Once more in the port, he cut through the back streets to the front, where he turned right. The bay was at its most beautiful, perhaps because the hard sun and burning air were exaggerating contrasts. David Swinnerton had wanted to remain among the beauty of the mountains, he would choose the bay . . .

The blast of a horn jerked his thoughts back to the present and he realized that the car had wandered out into the centre of the road. He pulled in to the side and a builder's van swept by; as it passed, he read the name on the side: Javier Ribas. Builders and property developers were the modern plutocrats, making so much money that they didn't know how to hide it all from the tax people . . . The van's right-hand blinker flashed and it turned off the road. Gone to Las Cinco Palmeras, he thought. Then did that mean the young couple had found the money? He hoped they had. Helen was someone who deserved to succeed.

He didn't consciously make the decision, yet he braked and also turned right. The yard behind the restaurant was, despite the heat, filled with energetic movement. Near the kitchen door, a concrete mixer was turning and a man was shovelling the last of a pile of sand into it; beyond, a second man was working at a plumber's bench which had been placed up against the building, to take advantage of the shade. The lorry had turned and was now backing. It came to a stop, the driver shouted to the man by the concrete mixer who unclipped the tail-board, the hydraulic ram slowly raised the loading bay and sand began to spill.

Alvarez left his car and walked round to the door of the kitchen. It looked as if every fixture inside had been ripped out or was being ripped out . . .

'It's a horrible mess, but it's wonderful!'

He turned to face a smiling Helen.

'The builder's promised by all the saints in every calendar that the work will be finished in time for the inspector to pass it by the end of the month. So we'll be able to open on time after all . . . You must have a drink to celebrate.'

'I wish I could, but I'm on my way to Playa Nueva . . .'

'You can't find the time to wish us luck?'

'Señora, when you speak like that I will be honoured and my cousin will just have to go without her smoked pork.'

'Great. So let's go round to the front and try to get away from the worst of the racket.'

As they walked round the building, she said: 'If you want to see a change in someone, look at Mike. There's none of that surly bad temper now. Of course, it was really all frustration.'

They reached the palm trees. She pointed at the several tables and chairs. 'They're new. I set them out to see what they look like. We could have made do with the old ones, but they were beginning to look shabby and the British worry more about that sort of thing than the food . . . Sit down and I'll get the drinks. Are you still drinking brandy or would you prefer something else?'

'A coñac would be fine, thank you.'

She left and went into the restaurant through the main doorway. He stared at the bay, enjoying the view of which he never grew tired . . . He heard the shrill whine of the van before he saw it turn on to the track and come down, to pass out of sight. Helen returned with a tray on which were two glasses. 'I think the señor has just arrived,' he said.

'I love it when you call him the señor; it sounds so very grand.' She chuckled as she sat. 'I told him yesterday that at night he ought to wear tails to give us a little touch of class. His reply was interesting but unrepeatable!' She passed one glass across. 'And speaking of the devil . . .'

Taylor came up to the table. 'Drinking again?'

'I fear so,' replied Alvarez.

'I told him he had to stay and celebrate,' said Helen.

'Quite right. And since two's a celebration, but three's an orgy, I'll join you. Just get myself a drink.' He went back into the restaurant. When he returned, he raised his glass. 'To our opening day. May it not be completely shambolic.'

'Why should it be?' she asked with mock indignation.

'Because, my darling cook, as I've tried to explain before, we are by the dictates of local custom obliged to offer free food and drink to all potential customers. And if there's a hungrier and thirstier man than a Mallorquin on a free tuck-in, it's a Britisher.'

'You'll have to make certain that there's never too much around at any one moment.'

'Easier said than done, especially with some of the free-loading Brits who live here. They can smell out an unopened bottle at half a kilometre.'

Alvarez said: 'The señora tells me that Javier has promised the work will be completed before the end of the month?'

'He has. And I've made it very clear that unless this promise is a damned sight more reliable than all his previous ones, I'll personally shoot him.'

'I'm very glad you managed to sort out your problems.'

'We didn't,' said Helen. 'It was . . .'

Taylor cut in. 'I was lucky enough to meet an old friend who loaned us the money.'

'And you were always trying to say that you'd been born under an evil star.'

'Maybe that star's regressed.'

'Will you put that down in writing and sign it? . . . Mike, when you say it was an old friend who lent you . . .'

He cut in a second time. 'In this case, I literally did bump into him. I was rushing to buy some washers, tripped, and all but sent him flying. Took us a second or two to recognize each other, then it was a case of commemorating the reunion at the nearest bar. He wanted to know what I was doing out here and I told him and being down in the dumps, I filled in most of the sordid details. He said his father had died a year or so back and left him a fortune and why shouldn't he lend me the money for as long as I needed at nil interest? . . . I know one shouldn't borrow from friends, but I just didn't have the courage to turn it down.'

'Who would, in such circumstances?' said Alvarez. He wished Taylor's interruptions had been more subtle and that Helen had not allowed her puzzled surprise to be so obvious. Then, he would not have started asking himself questions.

There were times when Alvarez wondered how he could be such a fool as not to leave well alone when he had the chance? If he'd reached a solution that seemed obviously correct, why worry about one small conflicting detail that was probably totally immaterial? What did it really matter if Taylor had given Helen a different version of events? He might have wanted to avoid admitting to her that he had borrowed the money from a friend. And yet it was somewhat difficult really to believe that . . . He sighed as he drove back to Puerto Llueso.

He parked in the square, close to the Caja de Ahorros y Monte de Piedad de Las Baleares, went inside, and asked to speak to the manager.

The manager said: 'You want to know about a large

cheque he may have received in the past few days?'

'That's right.'

'Could it be bad?'

'I doubt it.'

'Then why . . .?' The manager waited, but Alvarez said nothing. 'All right, I'll find out.' He used the internal telephone to speak to someone, replaced the receiver. 'It won't be a moment.' He cleared his throat. 'You wouldn't like to tell me what this is all about?'

'I'm not certain.'

'He's not been banking very long with us.'

'I don't suppose he has.'

'He's bought Las Cinco Palmeras, round the bay.'

'I know.'

'He's modernizing it and hopes to open quite soon.'

'Yes.'

'There was a problem about money for repairs and alterations.'

'I know.'

'Goddamn it, Enrique, you're being closer than a bloody oyster!'

'An oyster without a pearl.'

A man in his twenties, with a neatly trimmed, very dark beard, entered and put a sheet of paper down on the desk. The manager read what was written. 'Is that all we know?'

'At the moment. The cheque went to head office in the usual bag.'

The manager spoke to Alvarez. 'Last Saturday, he paid in a cheque for seven hundred thousand.'

'Who drew the cheque?'

'I can't answer. As you've just heard, it's gone to head office for clearing.'

'Will you find out?'

The manager nodded at the cashier, who dialled the main branch in Palma. He spoke briefly, replaced the receiver. 'They'll get back on to us.'

'Thanks.'

The cashier left. The manager asked how Alvarez's family was and for several minutes they chatted amiably. Then, the expected call came through.

'The cheque was on the Banco de Bilbao in Corleon and was signed by Señorita Benbury,' said the manager.

CHAPTER 23

Alvarez walked into the supermarket in Corleon and asked one of the two cashiers where Agueda was; he was directed through to the bread counter. There, he waited until the last customer had been served with a barra, then said: 'D'you remember me?'

Agueda was dressed even more flamboyantly than before and her fingers sparkled with jewellery; her make-up was less than subtle. 'Of course—the detective from Llueso who enjoys a good brandy. Let's go through to the office and see what we can find.' She called over an assistant—there was now another customer wanting bread—and came round the counter. 'So how's the tourist trade on the island this summer? Down a bit on last year?'

Speaking rapidly and commenting sarcastically on government policy, the greed of shop assistants, and the iniquities of IVA, she led the way into the office. She produced a bottle of Carlos I and two glasses, pushed the bottle across. 'I always leave the man to pour.'

He half filled the glasses, passed her one.

She drank, put her glass down on the desk. 'Now you can tell me what's brought you back here?'

'I'm trying to tie up a few loose threads.'

'It's a long way to come just to do that.'

'My boss is a very tidy-minded man . . . I wanted to have a word with Señorita Benbury, but when I went to her house

I couldn't get an answer. The maid wasn't in and the dog seems to have gone. Is she not living there any more?'

'I haven't heard she's left.'

'When did you last see her?'

She opened a drawer and brought out a box of cigars; she lit a match for both of them. 'It must have been the end of last week.'

'Was she on her own?'

'Pierre was with her, as usual.'

'She's still thick with him, then?'

'It's a funny thing about that.' She drew on the cigar, exhaled slowly and with pleasure. 'Like I told you before, she began by throwing herself at him. But recently, damned if it didn't look as if the boot's on the other foot.'

'How sure of that are you?'

'I don't reckon to have lived forty-one years without knowing who's doing the chasing.'

He thought it was probably more than forty-one years. 'Perhaps she's got fed up with him. Or else she's decided to play hard-to-get.'

'After what's happened?'

'Then what's the answer?'

'She's a bitch.'

'Whatever she is, I need a word with her.'

'One flutter of her eyelids and you can't keep away?'

'Maybe Pierre can say where she is now—where's he live?'

'Right at the back of the urbanización in a grotty little bungalow, although if you listened to him you'd think he owned the biggest house on the main canal. But at this time of the day, he'll be in a bar.'

'Any particular one?'

She shrugged her shoulders. 'Wherever the most foreign women are . . .'

*

Alvarez found Pierre Lifar in El Pescador, a large bar on the front road whose walls were decorated with many of the implements which the fishermen had used before the tourists had arrived and destroyed their trade. He had expected Lifar to be an Adonis, but found him to be a medium-sized man, knottily built, with a rugged face that spoke of strong living, strikingly blue eyes, and his only ostentation an unbuttoned shirt which displayed his hairy chest.

'I'm Pierre Lifar. So who are you?' He spoke Spanish fluently, rolling his R's with Gallic freedom.

'Inspector Alvarez, from Mallorca, of the Cuerpo General de Policía.'

'We've all got our problems.'

'Indeed. Shall we sit outside?'

'Is that an order?'

'A request, señor. You will have a drink?'

'I'll have a Ricard, even though my mother taught me to be beware of policemen who offered me drinks.'

Alvarez carried the glasses out to one of the tables which was in the shade of an overhead awning.

Lifar added water to his drink. 'What d'you want from me?'

'I need to speak to Señorita Benbury and I'm told you know where she is.'

'Then you've been told wrongly.'

'But you are very friendly with her?'

'And if I am?'

'Then you can probably tell me where I can find her.'

'I probably can't.' He sipped the milky liquid, put the glass down. 'What's your angle? Something to do with the car crash?'

'That's right.'

'Why? It's history.'

'Not yet. Señor Thompson was poisoned.'

'Christ!' Lifar stared at him in open-mouthed astonishment. 'Is that on the level?'

'He was poisoned with colchicine. This did not directly
kill him, but because it seriously affected him, he crashed
and was killed.'

'Are you suggesting Charlie knew anything about all
that?'

'If you're asking me if I suspect her of having administered
the poison, I know for certain she did not.'

'Then how does she come into it?'

'It is what happened after the accident that now interests
me.'

'I don't understand.'

'There is no need for you to.'

'You're bloody sharp, aren't you?'

'Just rather sad.'

'What the hell . . .?' He drank, bewildered and irritated.

'I need to know about your relationship with the señorita.'

'That's my business.'

'It is also mine.'

They stared at each other with silent hostility. Lifar, who
had begun by despising the shambling inspector, realized
that he was dealing with a far more determined character
than he had imagined. He also remembered that he had not
applied for a residencia, being unable to bring into the
country the minimum amount of money that was necessary.
'What d'you want to hear about?'

'Everything.'

He spoke with surly resentment. He hated having to
admit to a defeat and by referring to it he was reminding
himself of the possibility that from the beginning she had
been using him while all the time he'd believed he had been
going to use her.

He'd marked her out the first time he'd seen her—which
was hardly surprising since she was extravagantly beautiful.
He'd been surprised that she could appear to be so in love
with a man noticeably older than herself, but had been
satisfied that this could only work in his favour; certain

women initially were attracted by older men, but it was an attraction which seldom, if ever, managed to meet the determined challenge of someone young, vigorous, and irresistible, and then their passion was all the greater. So when her man was killed in a car crash, he'd been about to go after her when she'd thrown herself at him like crazy. Only . . .

'Only she wouldn't hop into bed with you?'

'I got all I wanted,' he answered defensively.

'You're lying.'

'How the hell would you know?'

Alvarez stared at the passing traffic for a time, then said: 'Did you know she's left?'

'Left where?'

'Corleon.'

'Who says she has?'

'So she just used you until the last moment, then cleared off without a word.'

Lifar finished his drink.

CHAPTER 24

As always, Alvarez was reluctant to enter a hospital, but he told himself he was being stupid and walked across to the reception and inquiry desk in the Clínica Bahía with what he hoped was an air of resolution. He told the middle-aged woman he wanted a word with someone in accounts and she directed him down the right-hand corridor.

Several patients were waiting to pay their accounts, or give the details of their medical insurances, but he was able to attract the attention of a man who took him through to the office behind the general area.

'You're inquiring about Señor Higham's account—what exactly is it that you want to know?'

'Whether he made any phone calls while he was here. You'd have a record of them, wouldn't you?'

'Yes, of course. They go on the bill.'

'Would anyone here know where he was calling?'

'Our only record is the number of pulses.'

'They should be enough. Can you find out the details?'

It took less than two minutes to turn up the details of the account.

'Señor Higham made three calls and they added up to seventy-one pulses.'

'You don't have the number for each call?'

'No, only the total.'

'What rates were they at?'

'One at full, one at normal, one at cheap.'

'If they were all local calls, they must have been long ones?'

The man smiled. 'Interminable, I'd say.'

'Thanks very much . . . There's one last thing. D'you mind if I telephone the British consulate?'

He spoke to the assistant consul and asked if Señor Higham had requested anyone in the consulate to help expedite the repayment of his stolen travellers' cheques? There had been no such request. To the best of anyone's memory, there had been no communication of any sort from Señor Higham.

Alvarez left the hospital and walked back to his car. He sat behind the wheel, lowered the windows, and switched on the fan to try and clear the heat. He knew exactly what Superior Chief Salas was going to say. An intelligent detective would have realized the truth long ago . . .

For several days after the crash, it had been impossible to know who the two victims were—their papers had been stolen, one of them was dead, the other was suffering from loss of memory. The doctors had been puzzled by that loss of memory because there had been no obvious head injuries serious enough to account for it; but what doctor could ever speak too dogmatically about the human brain?

Some days after the car accident, Higham's passport and wallet had been thrown into a street refuse container. This was a normal way of getting rid of incriminating evidence. But why had not the thief, or thieves, taken the opportunity to dispose of Thompson's things at the same time?

Back in the UK, Higham's wife had left him and he'd no relatives to whom he'd be able to turn for comfort or help. It was his first visit to the island. So whom had he been phoning from the Clínica Bahía? How had he paid his account in cash when all his money had been stolen and he'd not called on the consulate to help him gain a refund on the travellers' cheques?

There could be little doubt that Charlotte Benbury had been very much in love with Taylor. Yet within days of his death, she had thrown herself at Pierre Lifar. Only a bitch could act like that. Yet when he, Alvarez, had met her, he'd been sufficiently surprised and shocked that she should have acted as she had to begin constructing excuses for her; one might be shocked by the actions of a bitch, but surely seldom surprised, so somewhere within him there must have been doubt. A bitch would not have kept the photograph of the dead man on the dressing-table in her bedroom. Yet a woman who had loved deeply would surely have had a much better photograph than the one he had seen?

How had Charlotte known that Mike Taylor was so desperate for money? Why should she send him seven hundred thousand pesetas when she had never met him and might, such was human nature, easily be jealously resentful of him? And why had he tried to hide the fact that it was she who had given it to him when on the face of things there was no reason to do so?

Steven Taylor had been a man of charm and a golden tongue, with an inability to understand normal moral values. He'd made money by swindling people, been caught and convicted, yet by luck had escaped a prison sentence.

Even his conviction had not taught him discretion and later, after an impossible second marriage, he'd resumed his swindling ways. Disaster had threatened. The police were gathering the evidence to arrest him again and now he could be quite certain that he would be imprisoned. So he'd planned his 'death', successfully blackmailing his wife into financing it because his arrest and conviction would have shrivelled her snobbish soul.

Reborn in the name of Thompson, he'd resumed his old ways. He'd met Charlotte and had fallen wildly in love with her and, despite the difference in their ages, she had fallen equally in love with him.

He'd travelled to the island, possibly when temporarily short of funds and hoping against all the probabilities to get some more money out of his wife, and had met, in addition to her, his son and three potential victims. He'd set up a swindle and had sold shares in Yabra Consolidated to Wheeldon, Reading-Smith, and Valerie. Only this time, irony had played a hand. Instead of the shares being value-less, they'd suddenly become valuable. Inevitably, he'd set out to retrieve them and because of his golden tongue and a self-confidence that nothing seemed capable of denting, he'd succeeded. But for once his choice of victims had in part been bad. Reading-Smith was a self-made millionaire, contemptuous of any standards but those he set himself, ruthlessly convinced that his wealth set him apart from ordinary mankind. A man of his nature could never suffer being swindled without becoming determined to get his own back. Instinct had told him something about Thompson, a private detective had filled in the details. So when Thompson had returned, driven on by an inflated ego to sell him more shares, he'd bought them. And then made it clear that Thompson had just landed himself in trouble.

Thompson had considered the situation and very rapidly come to the conclusion that the only practical thing was for Charlotte and him to sell up and move out of Spain. Once they were in another country, living under different names, they should be safe.

Just as he'd misjudged the kind of man Reading-Smith was, so he'd misjudged the intensity of Valerie's emotions which, at times, had a trace of madness about them. And when she'd pleaded with him to give her the rest of the money that her shares had made, he'd not understood that it was love which drove her, not cupidity. Had he done so, he might have been warned. Then again, perhaps he would just have laughed.

On the Wednesday, he'd given Higham a lift. He was not only a good talker, but also a good listener (in his 'job', it was often just as important to listen as to talk) and by the time they'd stopped for lunch, he'd learned a lot about Higham's life. An attack of migraine had been threatening all day and he'd taken a second capsule, but it was the first one which had contained the poison. He'd drunk very little, leaving Higham to finish a bottle of wine on top of the pre-lunch drinks. By the end of the meal, Higham wasn't drunk, but neither was he sober.

They'd driven away from the restaurant. Almost immediately, Thompson had suffered the initial symptoms of colchicine poisoning. One attack had been followed by another and this second one had left him too ill to continue driving. So he'd changed places with Higham. By chance, he'd not fastened his seat-belt; feeling too ill to bother, probably.

Higham had never before driven on roads such as that one, with its acute bends, sharp, winding ascents and descents, and unguarded edges, and at a time when he'd needed all his wits they'd been befuddled by alcohol. He'd been going far too fast for the corner, had not braked in time, but had braked too violently when he did; he had failed to correct the ensuing skid. The car had gone over the edge. Thompson, unbelted, had been thrown clear; Higham, belted, had stayed with the car for the whole of the fall and had been killed.

Shock can do strange things to the system. It can even, to some extent, counter the effects of poisoning for a brief while. Thompson, injured though not seriously, overcame the poisoning which in any case could never have been fatal because Valerie had been unable to pack a sufficient amount of crushed pills into any one capsule, and began to think clearly enough to realize that if he was delayed on the island for any length of time, Reading-Smith would probably succeed in amassing sufficient evidence to ensure he was arrested. He also realized that now fate, and not design, had given him the chance to 'die' a second time and so escape that possibility. And he had a fortune waiting so that never again would he have to put himself at risk (always supposing he could forgo the pleasure of proving to himself just once more how brilliant he was).

Higham's wife had left him, he'd no immediate family alive, and no one in the UK expected, or particularly wanted, to hear from him, so he offered a perfect false identity. But somehow, the passports had to be switched . . .

Previously it had not been difficult for an expert to lift a photograph from one passport and paste it on to another, but the impressed strip of clear plastic had been expressly designed to prevent that and because of this there was no way in which, in his present circumstances, he could make the alteration. Yet if only there were time, there'd be no difficulty. In every major city there were men skilled enough to unbind a passport, swap pages, and then rebind it so that only the most detailed examination—and certainly not the normally casual one of an immigration official—would disclose what had happened. But even if not badly injured, he needed hospital treatment and the moment he entered into official hands, he'd have to declare his identity . . . Then he thought up a plan by which he could gain time.

He had gathered up the two passports, the wallets, and all the papers, and had hidden them near the scene of the crash. Then he had waited to be found and taken to hospital.

In hospital he'd simulated loss of memory. The doctors had been slightly surprised, but not suspicious; why should they be, when it was in his own interests, apparently, to remember who he was? He'd telephoned Charlotte, told her where everything was hidden and who to contact in Palma. She'd flown over from Barcelona, collected the passports, etc., paid to have the page switched, destroyed the remains of Thompson's passport. She'd dumped the passport of Higham, now bearing Thompson's photo, in a litter-bin, together with the emptied wallet. She'd returned to Corleon.

As Higham, he'd regained his memory. His passport confirmed his identity. He'd repeated all that Higham had told him in the car, giving it as the story of his own life. His one fear, of course, was that by ill chance someone on the island who knew him as Thompson would find him in the hospital under the name of Higham, but he was a gambler and correctly reckoned the odds were all in his favour. And the deception only had to remain good until he was fit enough to be discharged from hospital, whereupon he would vanish . . .

In the event, his gamble would have failed but for one factor—ironically, a factor which he had never taken into consideration; that was, the complex relationship which existed between his son and himself. If called upon to describe this, he probably would present it in much simpler terms from those Mike had employed; but then he saw the world as a much simpler place. Mike had both loved and hated him and because of the hate he had known guilt and remorse. It was the remorse which had made Mike lie when called upon to identify the exhumed body—realizing that his father was not dead but had made yet another switch with a dead man. Correctly assuming that this must be because he had again been swindling people and was in trouble in consequence, he had made the false identification in the hope of expiating at least a part of his guilt . . .

Perhaps the truth would never have surfaced had Charlotte not been so in love. Because, knowing how close to death he'd come, so luminous with relief that he'd escaped, she'd recognized that she could never convincingly simulate enough grief and thus the only alternative, if the fiction of his death was to be supported, was to act the part of a bitch . . .

Alvarez used a handkerchief to mop the sweat from his forehead. Did Steven Taylor even now appreciate why Charlotte made him the luckiest dead man alive?

Alvarez came to a halt in front of Ca Na Muña. He switched off the engine, pulled the handbrake hard on, and put the car into reverse gear as an added precaution. He climbed out.

Valerie stepped into the doorway of the house and stood there as he climbed the stone steps. She was looking old and rather feeble. 'I suppose you've come to arrest me? If I can have a few minutes to pack . . .'

'Señora, I am not here to do that,' he answered, as he crossed the narrow level.

'Why not?'

'Because Steven Taylor is still alive. The man who died was Señor Higham, a hitch-hiker who was actually driving at the time of the crash. Afterwards, Steven Taylor changed identities in order to disappear. While you can clearly still be charged with administering the poison with intent to murder, it would be necessary for a successful prosecution for him to come back and give evidence against you. I am quite certain he will never do that.'

She turned and looked up at the olive tree she called the Laocöon. 'He's still alive?' she said in a low, toneless voice.

What was her overriding emotion? Thankfulness that after all she had not murdered, or bitterness that the man who had robbed her of her chance of honouring her promise to her husband was still alive? Alvarez found he could not answer the question.

THE END